Sienna's Rescue
by Nikki Tate

Happy Birthday
Noëlle !

Best Wishes —
Nikki Tate

198

Canadian Cataloguing in Publication Data

Tate, Nikki, 1962-
  Sienna's Rescue

  (StableMates ; 4)
  ISBN 1-55039-093-7
  I. Title. II. Series.
PS8589.A8735S53 1998   jC813'.54   C98-910881-3
PZ7.T2113Si 1998

We acknowledge the support of the Canada Council
for the Arts for our publishing program.
We acknowledge the assistance of the Province of British Columbia,
through the British Columbia Arts Council.

Cover illustration © 1998 by Pat Cupples

Published by
SONO NIS PRESS
PO Box 5550, Stn. B
Victoria, BC V8R 6S4
sono.nis@islandnet.com
http://www.islandnet.com/sononis/

PRINTED AND BOUND IN CANADA

For Peter,
For your support and encouragement
when I needed it most.

And for Misty,
Who was afraid of imaginary snakes.

Chapter One

Jessa peered into the darkness, straining to see through the driving rain and into the shadows. She leaned out the open window of her little attic room, shivering in the cold rush of air. Wind tossed the glistening leaves and branches of the apple tree in her backyard.

The alarm clock on her bedside table said 3:10 a.m. *What noise had woken her?* Jessa pulled the window shut and crept back into bed. She wiggled down under the covers and snuggled deeper into the soft pillows. *It must have been a dream,* she decided, and closed her eyes.

A moment later an eerie cry rose over the steady drum of rain on the attic roof. The creepy sound was much louder than the ruckus of the spring storm that had been soaking southern Vancouver Island for two days. Usually Jessa loved the way the falling rain could lull her to sleep. But now, lying rigid in the darkness, her eyes widened and the fine hair on her arms stood straight up.

What was it?

1

The thin, warbling wail filled the room: a miserable cry of some kind of animal in pain.

Jessa crept to the window again, shuddering. She opened it wide and a spray of raindrops blew towards her with the next gust of wind.

She strained to hear, to make out something other than the swish and patter of rain in the trees. Faintly, something rustled in the bushes by the side of the house. Jessa's eyes widened and she backed away from the window until she felt the familiar round edge of her mattress behind her knees.

The wind lifted the edges of the loose papers on her desk as if a ghost were rifling through her things. Jessa's skin crawled as she slowly sat down on the edge of her bed. *What on earth was out in her backyard? A rat? No, too large. A cat? Or, maybe a raccoon?*

The only problem was, rats, cats and raccoons didn't wail like the animal she had heard. *A wolf? There were no wolves on Vancouver Island—or, were there?*

One thing Jessa did know for sure was there was no way to get back to sleep until she found out what was out there. And, if the monstrous creature wasn't going to show itself, Jessa would just have to march right downstairs and. . . .

Another wailing howl filled her room, much louder now that the window was wide open. *Why hadn't her mother woken up? Why had this THING chosen HER window to hide under?*

"Think, Jessa, think," she whispered to herself,

trying to keep her breathing steady and her heart from leaping out of her throat.

She weighed her options. If she stayed where she was, sitting stiffly on the edge of her bed, she would probably catch pneumonia and certainly not get any sleep.

If she crawled back into bed and somehow managed to trick herself into falling asleep, she would have hideous dreams and whatever sleep she might get wouldn't be worth having. If she woke her mother up to help investigate, Jessa would certainly get into trouble and, with her luck, whatever was lurking outside would have run away.

Jessa decided she had no option but to sneak downstairs and into the kitchen. There, she could grab the portable phone—just in case she had to call 911. Perhaps she would have a better view of the backyard from the kitchen window. If worst came to the worst, she could quickly open the back door and peek outside. . . .

Jessa shuddered at the thought. Somehow, having a plan emboldened her. She pulled on a sweater and quietly opened her bedroom door.

Once downstairs, she armed herself with the heavy black poker from the fireplace and fumbled to loosen the phone from its cradle. She crept to the kitchen window and peered out into the darkness beyond.

A blast of wind spattered rain against the window and Jessa jumped, her heart racing. Her whole body was rigid with the effort of listening, but all she could hear was the wind wrestling with the trees and the rain gurgling and slurping out of the drainpipe at the corner of the house like a small waterfall.

Obviously, whatever it was had gone, she reasoned, *or surely she would have heard the dreadful noise again.* With this in mind, she carefully opened the back door and looked outside. Before she could jump back, a large animal with flashing eyes leaped out from behind the chrysanthemum bush.

"Ahhh!" Jessa managed to cry out before the soaking wet dog pushed past her into the warmth of the kitchen.

Black and white and about the size of a small German Shepherd, the dog gave her a look which said, 'What took you so long?' For a long moment, they stood staring at each other and then the dog gave himself a hard shake, spritzing the whole kitchen. The dog's shaggy coat dripped muddy water all over the kitchen floor.

Jessa closed the back door. She kneeled down and the dog came straight to her, wagging his tail happily. The white tip on the long tail looked like a cheerful flag waving a salute to Jessa's hospitality. He had no collar or tag but seemed too friendly to be a stray or a wild dog. Jessa decided he must have an owner who was probably very worried about him.

"Shhh," she cautioned as she crept back upstairs to her room, the dog close at her heels. It seemed he had no intention of letting his rescuer out of his sight. "You can sleep here tonight," she said, patting the rug beside her bed. The dog didn't offer any argument. His black nose led him once around the room as he gave everything a quick sniff. Satisfied the place seemed a suitable place to stay, he returned to the rug, turned around in place three times, curled up in a little ball, heaved a deep sigh of relief and fell asleep.

Jessa watched him sleep, chin resting over his back leg, his tail covering his nose. His long, silky coat was beginning to dry and Jessa was starting to get very tired. She turned off the little lamp by her bed, pulled the covers over her head, and fell instantly into a deep and dreamless sleep.

Early the next morning, Jessa rolled over and stretched. She was startled when a wet lick slurped across the back of her hand.

"Good morning!" she said, grinning at the dog who had put his front paws up on the bed. She scratched behind the dog's ears and his tail waved slowly back and forth.

"We'd better go down and see if we can find you some breakfast," she said. Halfway down the stairs, Jessa stopped. *What was she going to tell her mother?*

Chapter Two

"Morning, most beautiful Mother," Jessa said walking into the kitchen, the dog at her heels. Before she had a chance to introduce her companion, he bounded across the kitchen and jumped at her mother in an exuberant greeting.

Jessa's mother shrieked and dropped her teacup which smashed on the kitchen floor. The dog was unperturbed—his tail wagged furiously and he yipped twice with the excitement of meeting another new person.

Jessa's mother backed up against the counter and tried to push the dog away with one hand while she clutched at her heart with the other.

"Sorry! Sorry!" said Jessa, scrambling to catch the dog and pull him away.

"What the heck is going on here?" Jessa's mother managed to gasp. From the look of horror on her face, Jessa could see her mother was less than thrilled with their surprise house guest. "Would you care to explain?"

"I think he's hungry," Jessa said as she hunted

through the cupboards for something to give the dog for breakfast.

"Hungry?" her mother asked, flabbergasted.

Quickly, Jessa filled her mother in on the adventures of the night before. "I'll phone the dog pound right after breakfast," she added hastily. "I'm sure somebody is looking for him. Isn't he cute?"

Her mother picked up the pieces of the broken cup. "Cute? He smells. You nearly scared me to death letting him attack me like that."

"He didn't attack you! He's just very . . . outgoing."

Jessa's mother remained unimpressed. "He can't stay."

"Why not? We have room. He's housebroken . . . I think." Jessa opened the back door and the dog ran outside. A moment later he trotted back in looking quite pleased with himself. "See?"

"Look, Jessa, he almost certainly has a home. I'll call the radio station and see if anyone has reported him missing. They have a 'found pet alert', too. I'll let them know we've found a dog. Does he have a collar?"

"No. I checked already." Jessa put a big bowl of cereal and milk down on the floor. The dog greedily slurped at the delicious meal.

"The poor thing is starving," said Jessa's mother.

"I'll give him a bath if he can stay—just until we find his owner," Jessa pleaded. "He would be so miserable at the pound. He's as good as gold. He didn't make a sound all night. You can hardly blame him for being so friendly after he had to spend who knows how long out in that terrible storm. Please?"

Susan Richardson looked from her daughter to the black and white dog who was pushing the empty bowl across the kitchen floor with his nose, still licking, trying to get every last drop. She sighed heavily and swept up the smaller pieces of china.

"Fine. Just for the weekend. He can't stay here alone while you're at school. Why don't you take him to the store and buy some real dog food. I don't want him throwing up because we're feeding him the wrong stuff."

Looking at the dog's wagging tail, Jessa didn't think he was too unhappy with his bowl of Rice Puffers. "Thank you!" she said, and ran upstairs to rummage through the bottom of her closet for something she could use as a leash. She found an old lead shank of Rebel's and ran back downstairs.

"Breakfast!" her mother admonished before she could tie the rope around the dog's neck and flee out the door.

This is so great, Jessa thought to herself as she and her temporary dog walked down the street together. She had wanted a dog for as long as she could remember. Almost as much as she had wanted a horse. Her mother was always telling her that if she wanted something badly enough, the universe had a way of providing—if only for the weekend.

That had certainly been the case with Rebel, her

pony. Out of the blue, her mother had heard about a Welsh-Quarter Horse cross available on a free lease. The next thing Jessa knew, Rebel had moved into a stall at Dark Creek Stables, a small barn not far from her house in Kenwood.

Jessa cleaned stalls and helped old Mrs. Bailey around Dark Creek in exchange for Rebel's board. It was a lot of work, especially during the school year, but there wasn't much else she'd rather be doing. She had often thought that a dog would be a great addition to the scenario, a buddy while she mucked out stalls or headed off on a trail ride with Rebel.

Unfortunately, her mother wasn't much of a pet person. She had a little greenhouse, a lovely garden and about a zillion houseplants. Jessa couldn't understand how anyone could be so crazy about growing green things, which all looked more or less the same to her. Something warm and furry you could actually play with was much more fun.

"Whoa," said Jessa to the dog who was walking about two metres ahead of her and nearly pulling her arm out of its socket. "Slow down. Heel!" The dog paid no attention to her whatsoever. Jessa sped up. The dog walked faster. Jessa broke into a jog. The dog got very excited and started to run. He nearly pulled Jessa off her feet. "Whoa! Hang on! Stop!" Jessa dug in her heels and hauled the dog to a stop. "Sit."

The dog stood looking up at her, wagging his tail and panting. Whoever had owned him before hadn't taught him much. Jessa reeled in the slack of the leash and set off again. The dog pulled and pulled and made terrible choking noises until Jessa was convinced he was hanging himself. The trip to the store took much longer than usual and by the time she had tied the dog to the bicycle rack, her arms felt all rubbery.

Going home was even harder. Somehow Jessa managed to juggle the bag of dog food, a bottle of milk and her exuberant companion.

"How did it go?" her mother asked when they came in the back door.

"Fine," Jessa said grimly, dropping the bag of food on the floor. The dog sniffed it.

"I called the pound and the radio station," her mother said. A fist formed in Jessa's stomach. Quickly, she tore open the bag of dog food and poured some in a bowl. Maybe if she fed him and made him feel at home, nobody would claim him. Deep down, she knew her logic didn't make sense.

"Nobody has reported a missing dog."

Jessa breathed a sigh of relief. "Too bad," she said, trying not to sound too gleeful. "Well, I'd better get ready to go down to the barn. The dog and I can walk."

"Jessa?"

Jessa stopped at the bottom of the stairs. No doubt her mother was going to try and stop her from taking the dog to Dark Creek Stables. She quickly thought up a couple of great arguments. She imagined a long, quiet trail ride with her faithful companion trotting along at Rebel's heels.

"Maybe you should give him a name—a temporary name instead of calling him 'the dog' all the time."

"How about Patches?" Jessa asked.

"What about Romeo?" her mother countered. "After all, he did serenade you in the middle of the night."

"Romeo?" Jessa thought it was a dumb name for a dog. On the other hand, she figured she'd better encourage her mother to bond with the visitor. Giving him a name was an excellent start. "Okay. Romeo it is."

"Don't get too attached to him, Jessa," her mother warned.

"I know, I know."

"I'll give you two a ride. You can walk home later."

When Jessa swung her feet out of their rattletrap car and stood in front of the little barn at Dark Creek Stables, she felt instantly relaxed and happy. There was no place on earth she would rather be. Jessa's mother drove off down the long driveway leaving Jessa and the dog standing side by side in the little parking area.

Romeo tipped his nose up, savouring the scents of horses and manure, hay and chickens. He snuffled as he breathed, intent on drinking in all the delicious smells of the barnyard.

When three of Mrs. Bailey's hens clucked by, Romeo quivered with excitement, his whole body taut with anticipation. The brownish red hens paid no attention to him at all. Romeo didn't appreciate being ignored. He let out a loud yelp and lurched forward, plunging after the retreating chickens.

The leash jerked out of Jessa's hands. "Romeo!" she cried out.

Romeo obviously had only one thing in mind—devouring the tasty hens, a plump and promising group just centimetres in front of his snapping teeth.

"Romeo! Come! Come here right now!" Jessa shouted.

The chickens squawked and flapped wildly as they tried to leap into the air. With a great rush of fluttering wings and a chorus of high-pitched cuckles, the hens flew awkwardly in all directions. One flew over the half-door of a box stall. Romeo stood barking hysterically outside the door, scratching to get in. Luckily, Jasmine, the usual resident of the stall, was out in her paddock when the frantic hen dropped in.

"You bad dog!" Jessa said, picking up the end of the rope.

"Any dog who will not immediately come when called has no place on a farm and definitely not out on the trail!"

"Mrs. Bailey!" said Jessa, shocked. "I didn't see you. . . ."

"Are you dog-sitting? This is no place for a dog who knows nothing about farm animals," Mrs. Bailey grumped. The older woman usually looked stern. At the moment, she looked furious. She opened the stall door and clucked softly to her hen.

"Come on, Izzie. There's a good girl."

Izzie stalked haughtily out of the stall. She gave Romeo a beady glare with her sharp black eyes.

The dog muffled a bark and whined. Jessa held onto the improvised leash with both hands, hoping the knot would hold.

"He's a stray," said Jessa. "We're just looking after him until we find his owner."

"Well, don't let go of that rope. Either tie him up or lock him in a stall. A dog like that is dangerous. I can't have him chasing the horses or the chickens. Besides, he could very easily get kicked if he's not careful, and it wouldn't be good if his owner claimed a dog with a broken back."

Jessa hadn't thought of that. Her vision of a faithful companion on the trails was disappearing quickly. Well, like it or not, Romeo would have to learn some manners before he was going to be able to join her in doing anything fun.

Later that morning, when Jessa and Rebel rode off down the long driveway, Romeo was left locked in a stall. He was not impressed. Jessa could hear his piteous howls all the way to the start of the Dark Creek Railway Trail. Her heart ached for him as she urged Rebel into a brisk trot. She hoped Mrs. Bailey was out of earshot. *Somehow,* she decided, *she had to find a way to teach Romeo how to behave.*

"Hurry up in there, Jessa!"

"I'm brushing my teeth!"

Monday mornings were the worst of the whole week. At the best of times, Jessa didn't think much of getting up early, especially when it meant going to school.

Despite what her mother said about her deliberately dawdling, Jessa really did try to hurry. It didn't help that on this particular Monday morning Jessa was extra tired because of the long argument she and her mother had had about Romeo the night before.

Jessa had insisted he would be safest staying with them until his owner showed up. Her mother felt he should wait at the dog pound. Bursting into tears had only made her mother angry and she paid no attention when Jessa sobbed that they might as well send Romeo to jail, abandoned again. After a whole weekend without a single phone call about the missing dog, Jessa was secretly beginning to hope Romeo's owners didn't want him any more.

"Jessa! I'm going to be late for work!"

In the end, it had been an early morning call from the temporary employment agency that had saved Romeo a trip to the dog pound. Jessa's mother went to school part-time where she was studying to be an accountant. She provided bookkeeping services for a few small businesses and worked at offices when the agency could find her jobs. The unexpected call this morning meant she didn't have time to take Romeo anywhere.

Jessa hurried out of the bathroom.

"I'll run home at lunch to take him for a quick walk," Jessa said as her mother closed the bathroom door.

"Fine!" she called.

"How long will this job last?" Jessa asked through the closed door.

"At least a week and maybe two."

Jessa grinned. She kneeled down and hugged Romeo. "Great!" If her mother were distracted with work, maybe she wouldn't be so determined to get rid of Romeo right away.

Jessa picked up her school bag. She filled Romeo's food and water bowls and ran out the back door.

"See you at lunch!" she called back to the window where Romeo's black nose pressed against the glass.

Chapter Three

"And in local news this morning, the Kenwood Animal Rescue Society has seized a number of animals from a Saanich Peninsula farm. Two goats, a pig, and several horses were among the animals found neglected and abandoned and which are now in the care of the Society."

Jessa rolled over in bed, half dozing, as she listened to C-FIX radio. A woman's voice came on the air. "The animals were in a terrible state when our volunteers were called to the scene by police," she said. "The horses are suffering from severe malnutrition, foot problems and a variety of health concerns."

The announcer continued. "Yannic Wolfe of the Kenwood Animal Rescue Society says the animals have been temporarily moved to the rehabilitation facility on West Coast Road. Officials say that after a brief assessment period, foster homes will be required to nurse these animals back to health."

Jessa opened her eyes and looked up at the giant poster stuck to the ceiling above her bed. An

Andalusian stallion danced across a cobblestone courtyard, a well-muscled animal in peak condition. She hated to think what the abused horses they were talking about on the radio might look like.

"Yuck!" she groaned as a wet tongue slithered between her fingers. She pulled her hand back from where it hung over the edge of the bed.

"Come on, Romeo. Up you get!"

Romeo didn't hesitate and jumped up beside her. He put his chin on Jessa's chest and thumped his tail on the bedspread. She couldn't quite believe they had actually survived a whole week together. She hadn't even minded giving up her lunch hours in order to take the dog for a quick run.

A couple of times her best friend Cheryl had come along and they had eaten their lunches under the apple tree in the backyard. Romeo loved cheese sandwiches but didn't think too much of grapes. Those he rolled around on his tongue for a while and then carefully spit them out.

Jessa closed her eyes and idly scratched the dog behind his ears. A long, heavy sigh and more tail thumping indicated she was scratching Romeo in just the right place.

"Jessa?"

Jessa jerked awake at the sound of her mother knocking on her bedroom door. She hadn't even realized she had dropped back off to sleep.

Romeo lifted his head and barked a menacing, 'woof'. The bedroom door swung open. "Jessa, you are going to be . . . Jessa!"

17

"Get off, Romeo," Jessa said, pushing at the dog who had suddenly become a floppy, boneless sack of fur.

"What did I tell you about keeping him off the bed?"

"Off!" Jessa said sternly, pushing harder. "Down. Bad dog."

Romeo ignored her efforts completely. He stretched his head up until it was resting on Jessa's pillow.

"Oh, Mom. Look! He's so sweet!"

"That is not sweet! Oh, no!" her mother exclaimed. "Your rug!"

Jessa sat up in bed and looked where her mother was pointing.

"Oh-oh," she said guiltily, even though she had done nothing wrong.

Long strands of coloured fabric lay in feathery strips across the floor. Jessa had a thick, braided rug on the wooden floor of her little attic room. At least, there had been a nice rug on the floor when she had gone to bed the night before. The rug was no longer neat and oval, but frayed and shredded.

"What a mess, young lady! Jessa Marie Richardson, get up right now and clean this up!"

Jessa jumped out of bed. She wasn't going to argue. So far, at least, her mother hadn't threatened to cancel this morning's dog training class and send Romeo to the pound to pay for his crime.

"And hurry up! Since you and that dog have slept so late, you're both going to be late for obedience school. And goodness knows, that dog needs some training!"

Jessa listened to her mother's footsteps retreating down the narrow staircase. Jessa had almost forgotten about the class. She had argued all week that just in case the dog's owner never showed up, that it would be easier to find Romeo a good home if he had some basic training. Of course, in Jessa's mind, she was thinking that if she could prove Romeo was capable of being well behaved, her mother might actually let her keep him.

It had been quite a fight to convince her mother. In the end, Jessa had to agree to wash and dry the dishes every night for the next month before her mother finally relented and signed the two of them up for a set of basic classes.

She gathered what she could of the shredded bits of rug and threw them into the garbage can. The strips that were still attached to the edges of the rug, she tucked underneath and hid them as well as she could.

Romeo watched her work with one eye, his head still resting on the pillow.

"Come on, lazybones. Walk time!" Jessa retrieved Romeo's new leash and collar from her desk. At the mention of the word, 'walk', Romeo's ears pricked up and he bounded off the bed, his tail wagging.

"That was quick!"

"We jogged." Jessa didn't tell her mother that it

was impossible to walk with Romeo pulling at the end of the leash. They had made it around the block in record time, despite Romeo's investigation of trees, telephone poles and fire hydrants.

"You had better work hard with that dog or we'll have to find someone else to look after him until his owner shows up. I don't know what we're going to do if he's going to chew things."

"We could get him a big bone at the pet store. I have enough allowance saved up for that. I'm sure it's just a phase," Jessa added much more confidently than she felt.

"A phase? Well, I don't know about that. But a bone isn't a bad idea."

"Mom, what if his owner never calls?" Jessa asked cautiously. "Could we *please* keep him?"

"Jessa, you know we have no time for a dog. Between school and riding. . . ."

"When he's trained, I can take him to the barn and he'll come with me on trail rides and . . . and protect me."

"From what?"

"Well, if I ever fell off, he could run for help. Like Lassie."

Susan Richardson put her hands on her hips and looked at her daughter for a long moment. "You have a great imagination, Jessa, I'll give you that. I'm sure sooner or later the owner will call to claim him. Maybe they're away and don't even know he's gone missing."

Jessa's mother held up a sign she had made on the computer.

FOUND:

MEDIUM-SIZED BLACK AND WHITE
MALE DOG IN KENWOOD
PLEASE CALL:
555-7294 TO CLAIM

"I'm going to take copies to the vet, the pet store and the *Kenwood Star News*. Surely somebody will see the poster and know where he belongs."

Here, thought Jessa. *Romeo belongs here.* But she didn't say anything as she sat down at the kitchen table for breakfast. *What point was there in antagonizing her mother?* Jessa would take Romeo to obedience classes and work harder than anyone else. She would prove that Romeo was quite capable of becoming an upstanding doggy citizen and a valuable member of the Richardson household.

Chapter Four

Twenty minutes into the first class, Jessa was ready to give up on the whole idea of dog training. The minute Romeo spotted the other dogs, he went berserk. He yapped and howled and completely ignored all Jessa's efforts to keep him quiet.

He wasn't the only dog misbehaving. The rag-tag group of twelve dogs and their frazzled owners spread out on the back field of the Kenwood Elementary School. A man with a megaphone shouted instructions over the incessant barking.

"Shhh. No!" said Jessa firmly, giving Romeo's leash a sharp tug, just like the instructor said. Romeo stopped barking, but only long enough to take a deep breath and gather his strength for a new round of whining and yapping.

"My name is Rodney Blenkinsop. Patience and consistency will be critical to your success. Even one yap is a yap too many!"

While Rodney was shouting instructions, his assistant, a young woman with frizzy hair and a big grin handed out coiled lengths of yellow, nylon rope. Each long rope had a snap on one end.

"Your fifteen metre line will be your best friend during this training course," said Rodney, stepping around a little black poodle who seemed to think hopping up and down on his back legs like a bunny was a respectable way for a dog to behave.

At least Romeo didn't act like a rabbit, Jessa thought, watching her dog bark excitedly at a big yellow Labrador retriever with a red kerchief tied around his neck. The dog's owner had a rather large belly and wore a matching bandanna around his throat. Jessa thought the pair of them looked ridiculous. The lab, however, was not barking.

During the class, the group learned the correct way to put training collars on their dogs and how to start working with the long, yellow leashes. Throughout the session, Rodney fed his new students a steady stream of encouragement.

When it was finally time to leave, Rodney spoke to each owner as the dogs filed out the gate at the bottom of the field.

"Don't forget to practise," he said to Jessa as he handed her a small sample bag of dog kibble. "You'll only get out of this class as much as you put in."

"Get in here," Jessa said, dragging Romeo into the box stall. "Come on!"

Romeo knew better. He planted all four feet firmly and refused to budge. Jessa had tied him to a fence post while she groomed and tacked up Rebel. With the exception of an occasional whining yelp, he had been pretty good. But now, she wanted to go on a trail ride, which meant leaving Romeo locked in a box stall.

"It's for your own good," she insisted, nearly pulling him off his feet. Romeo lay down in the dirt and glared at her defiantly.

Tears stung at the back of Jessa's eyelids. *Dogs weren't supposed to be such a nuisance.* In desperation, Jessa fished her cheese sandwich out of her back-pack and tore off a little piece. Romeo licked his lips and inched forward. Jessa gave him the piece of bread and cheese.

"Come on, Romeo. That's a good boy," she coaxed, another tasty morsel held out in her hand. She walked backwards into the stall. Romeo followed the cheese and bread.

The minute he was inside, she threw the rest of the sandwich into the far corner and when he chased it, she slipped out of the stall and closed the door. The howl of misery was so piteous, the world might have thought she was beating him.

"Romeo! Shhhh. I'll be back soon," she said. But the dog was inconsolable. All the way down to the end of the driveway she could hear his mournful cries.

With the echo of her dog's unhappiness ringing in her ears, it was impossible for Jessa to relax and enjoy her ride. Rebel was in fine spirits and sprang happily into a light canter when Jessa urged him along the Dark Creek Railway Trail. The leafy green bushes and trees on either side of the sheltered trail whirred past in a blur as they flew along.

The steady rhythmic drum of his hooves drilling a pattern into the ground comforted her. As soon as she pulled him up and they continued along at a walk, her troubled thoughts returned. *What was she going to do with that dog?* He was driving her crazy. And yet, when she was at school and he was at home, or now, while she was out enjoying a ride and he was back at the barn, she didn't feel quite right.

It was crazy. A dog, who wasn't even hers, who had only been around for a little more than a week, had already taken up residence in her heart.

Jessa cut her ride short and turned Rebel back towards the barn. He seemed a little surprised, but didn't argue. He practically danced along the trail, his head and tail lifted high. *At least one of us is having a good time*, Jessa thought ruefully.

Jessa didn't even wait for Rebel to come to a complete halt in front of the barn before she hopped off and ran her stirrups up.

"Romeo?" she called. An uneasy silence answered her. There was no sound from the box stall. Quickly, Jessa threw Rebel's halter on over his bridle and snapped him into the crossties. "Romeo!"

The stall door was still closed. Jessa ran and looked in over the door. "Romeo?" The stall was empty. She tore the door open and stepped inside, blinking in the dim light. She walked around the inside of the stall. There was truly no dog any-where. There was truly no dog any-where.

She whirled around and ran back outside, calling frantically. "Romeo! Where are you?"

But her dog was nowhere to be seen. Mrs. Bailey's hens clucked by in a row, unruffled. She wished she could understand their murmuring. If they had seen a black and white dog, they weren't telling.

"Romeo?" Jessa jogged down to the end of the driveway and looked both ways along the road. No Romeo.

She ran back up the driveway towards the barn, calling at the top of her lungs. "Romeo! Come here, boy!"

The door to the tack room swung open and Mrs. Bailey stepped out. "You sure are noisy. What's all the yelling about?"

"My . . . my . . . " Jessa's voice trembled. "Romeo got out and he ran away and he doesn't know where my house is and what if he goes up as far as the highway and. . . ." Jessa couldn't bear to think of what might happen.

"You mean, this Romeo?" Mrs. Bailey stepped to the side and Romeo stuck his head out of the tack room. "He was making such a din I could hear him all the way up at the house! I rescued him from jail and took him with me up into the hayloft. He gave me a hand sorting through the blankets. I have to take the soiled ones in to Suzanna at the tack store, to get them cleaned."

Jessa wasn't at all interested in hearing about Mrs. Bailey's plans for cleaning horse blankets. She ran to Romeo and threw her arms around his neck. He gave her a wet slurpy kiss on the cheek.

"He's awfully loud," remarked Mrs. Bailey with a sniff.

Jessa turned around when she heard the sound of truck tires scrunching in gravel.

"Hi Marjorie," Mrs. Bailey called cheerfully.

Marjorie eased herself out of her pickup truck and strode over to say hello. She was very short, not much taller than Jessa. Somehow, she seemed a lot taller than she really was. There was something tough and demanding about her, even though she was shaped a bit like an apple. Her stubby legs and roundish bottom were amazing in the saddle. She and her lovely Morgan mare, Toyland Babe were familiar to all the riders in the local show circuit.

"Barbara, did you hear?"

"Marjorie, I'm not psychic. Hear what? About the blanket cleaning special down at Oh Suzanna's Tack and Feed?"

"No. About the abused horses."

"Oh, I heard about them on the radio this morning," piped up Jessa. With all the traumatic events with Romeo, she had completely forgotten. "The Animal Rescue Society took them away . . . they were all sick and stuff."

"Tragic," pronounced Marjorie.

Mrs. Bailey stepped out into the sunshine and tipped her cowboy hat back. "Some people shouldn't be allowed to have horses." She spat in the dirt for emphasis. No matter how often Jessa saw Mrs. Bailey spit, she could not get used to it. Grown-ups, especially old grown-up women, were simply not supposed to do that.

"It's disgusting all right," said Marjorie. "Those poor animals. They hadn't been fed properly for months, that's what I heard."

Mrs. Bailey shook her head. "Disgusting is right."

"So?" said Jessa.

"So . . . what so?" asked Mrs. Bailey.

"So, why don't you bring them here? I heard they need foster homes because the Animal Rescue farm doesn't have room for them."

"We can't bring them here! We already have five horses. We don't have room for any more!"

"Well, how about just one of them? There's the second stall in the small barn. We could move the tractor into the shavings shed."

The two women looked at each other, and then at the small barn. The main barn at Dark Creek had four box stalls. Jasmine, Mrs. Bailey's pride and joy, lived in one of them. Toyland Babe had another and the last two stalls were taken by two more boarders, Brandy, a pinto gelding, and Billy Jack, an old gelding of unknown breeding who Jessa considered to be one of the ugliest horses she had ever met.

The second, smaller barn had just two stalls. Rebel stayed in one of them. The other stall was empty except for Mrs. Bailey's ancient tractor.

"Well, I don't know," said Mrs. Bailey slowly.

"You know," said Marjorie. "Jessa has a point. I know they were looking for places to keep the horses until they were well enough to adopt out."

"Yeah, foster homes. We could do that here, couldn't we?"

"It's an extra stall to clean and an extra mouth to feed. . . ."

Jessa interrupted quickly. "I don't mind. It wouldn't take me that much longer."

"I could give you a hand," offered Marjorie. "We were awfully quick to criticize—don't you think we should be just as quick to offer a helping hand?"

Mrs. Bailey couldn't seem to think of a compelling argument. The next thing Jessa knew, they had all piled into Marjorie's truck. Romeo sprawled awkwardly across Mrs. Bailey's lap, his head hanging out the window as he snuffled in the breeze.

Chapter Five

Romeo bounced out of the truck the minute Mrs. Bailey opened her door.

"Hey, you klutz," said Mrs. Bailey as Romeo's tail swished across her face. "That dog of yours has no manners."

Jessa could hardly argue. She trailed along behind her two older companions, firmly holding onto Romeo's leash.

The Kenwood Animal Rescue Centre was not a large facility, but everything about it was neat and tidy. Jessa stopped in front of a large sign with a map of the small farm. Each building on the property was named after a kind of tree.

'Dogwood', according to the map, housed dogs. 'Arbutus' was the residence for retired cats and 'Sitka' was for smaller farm animals like sheep and goats. Ducks, geese and injured birds resided in 'Hemlock'.

'Cedar' was the name of the main barn. By the time Jessa had located the barn on the map, Mrs. Bailey and Marjorie were out of sight. The barn lay at the end of a short trail that wound through a stand of pine trees.

Jessa ran to catch up.

"Stop it!" she said to Romeo who thought running was an invitation to jump up and bite the leash. He bounced around like an out-of-control furball, snapping at the leash and grinning wickedly.

"Romeo, stooo . . . ahhh!" Jessa tried to leap over her dog when he danced in front of her feet. There was no hope of recovering her balance. Jessa sprawled face first in the dirt.

"Oof," she said as Romeo planted his paws on her chest and started wagging his tail furiously. "Stop it!" Jessa's scolding trailed off into a dribble of giggles. Romeo's licking grew more frantic as Jessa tried to push him away. She was laughing so hard she could barely breathe.

She finally managed to roll over and push herself onto her knees. Romeo pawed at her, eager to continue their game.

"That's enough, you . . . you. . . ." She couldn't think of a suitable name to call the mutt who stood beside her, his head tipped to one side, a cheeky smirk on his black and white face.

"You good dog," she said, giving in and scratching him behind the ear. She was glad nobody from dog training class had witnessed Romeo's terrible manners.

When Jessa finally joined the others at the Cedar Barn, a young woman with dark brown hair had joined Mrs. Bailey and Marjorie. She wore jeans and a green shirt with 'Kenwood Animal Rescue Society' written in white letters across the back. There was a picture of a dog, a cat, and a donkey on the front of her shirt.

"Hi. You must be Jessa. My name is Yannic Wolfe. Your dog is welcome to visit, but you must keep him on a leash. Oh, and you should also keep well away from Dogwood. Some of the animals we get in here are pretty sick. I sure wouldn't want him to catch anything."

Yannic kneeled down and gave Romeo a friendly pat on the head. Romeo liked her right away. He put both front paws on her leg and gave her a wet kiss on the cheek. To Jessa's relief, Yannic wasn't the least bit annoyed.

"What a friendly dog," she said. When she stood up, Jessa noticed two muddy paw prints on the young woman's otherwise clean jeans. Yannic either didn't notice or she didn't mind.

"So, let's go look at the horses, shall we?" she asked.

The four horses shared a large paddock behind the barn. Each looked more run down than the next. A palomino gelding stood near the gate, his head hanging low, his ribs obvious through his dull coat. Yannic ducked between two rails and into the paddock.

"Old Sandy here, he's pretty quiet." The horse barely lifted his head as Yannic ran her hand over his protruding hip bones. "He's got a kind eye, this one. The farrier was out earlier and trimmed the hooves of the three geldings." She straightened up and looked across the paddock to where a fourth horse stood. "He didn't want anything to do with that little mare."

"What's wrong with her?" Mrs. Bailey asked, peering out from under the brim of her big, black cowboy hat.

"What isn't?" Yannic sighed. "I don't know what we're going to do with her. She's horribly under-weight—well, you can see that—her feet are in bad shape, she's got worms like you wouldn't believe. She has an infected cut over her eye—but worse than all that, she has quite an attitude."

"Can you blame her?" Marjorie asked.

Yannic shook her head. "We're told she's only four. Who knows what she's already been through? You can't really get near her. She doesn't trust a soul."

Jessa stood by the fence and watched the mare swishing her matted, clumpy tail. She couldn't even tell what colour the horse was supposed to be.

"What's her name?" she asked.

"Sienna."

"A pretty name for an ugly horse," remarked Mrs. Bailey. "Looks like trouble to me."

The little mare's gaze never left them. Every time someone moved, she noticed. Her head lifted a little and her ear flicked.

"So, you're looking for temporary homes for these horses?" Marjorie asked.

Yannic nodded. "The only horses we keep here are a few geriatric cases who won't ever be ridden again. But we don't have the space, or, quite frankly, a lot of money to keep seized horses like these here while they are nursed back to good health. That's why we try and find good foster homes."

"What happens then?" Marjorie asked.

"Sometimes the people who take them on wind up adopting them. We have quite a list of people who are willing to adopt once the horses are in good health. The potential adopters have to go through quite a long process before we hand them a horse. Not everyone has the right idea about the kind of horse they are going to get. The last thing we want is for horses like this to be passed from owner to owner."

Jessa couldn't stop staring at Sienna. *What kind of person would be willing to take on a horse who was barely alive and wouldn't even let you come close enough to help?*

"What are those marks?" Jessa asked.

"On her flanks? They're pretty well healed up now. It looks like she was beaten, maybe with a chain." Yannic shook her head slowly. "It's very sad when horses are treated this badly."

A queasy feeling settled in the pit of Jessa's stomach. *If they didn't help Sienna, who on earth would?*

Chapter Six

Mrs. Bailey narrowed her eyes and looked from horse to horse, studying each. "Let me think about this for a day or two," she said. "It's a big job to take on one of these animals."

Jessa trailed behind Mrs. Bailey and Marjorie as they made their way back towards the truck. Romeo seemed a little more subdued than usual, as if sensing the serious nature of the visit.

"I just don't know, Marjorie. I don't know if I have the energy to put into another horse."

"I could do some extra work," Jessa offered.

"I wonder if that old Sandy would get along with Billy Jack? I could turn them out together in the big field. Of course, the poor guy probably hasn't seen grass in a long time. We'd have to work him up to that slowly."

"What about Sienna?" Jessa asked.

Mrs. Bailey looked back over her shoulder and frowned. "Too much work." She turned back to Marjorie and the two women kept talking about what would be involved with taking one of the geldings.

"Exactly," muttered Jessa. Turning Sienna into the kind of horse someone would like to adopt wouldn't be easy.

"What happens if the horses don't get adopted?" Jessa asked as they reached the truck.

Marjorie looked back towards the barn.

"I suppose a really tough case would have to be put down."

"Is Sienna a tough case?" Jessa asked.

The two women exchanged a serious look. Mrs. Bailey stared down at the toe of her cowboy boot.

"Maybe," she said. "But Jessa, we don't really have time to work with a horse like Sienna."

Jessa didn't say anything. There was something in the tone of Mrs. Bailey's voice that said she was considering the mare's chances.

Jessa clucked to Rebel. She had rushed to the barn right after school so she'd have time to ride before dinner.

She balanced her sturdy bay pony in the corner and then sent him forward, squeezing with her legs and keeping her hands soft and steady.

"Come on, Rebel," she urged, asking him to lengthen his stride.

Rebel responded by sailing down the long side of the outdoor riding ring at Dark Creek Stables. Jessa grinned as she shortened his stride slightly in the corners and then sent him floating forward again on the long side. Few ponies had an extended trot as dynamic as his.

After her ride, Jessa led Rebel back to the barn. She had just snapped the crossties to his halter when Mrs. Bailey appeared.

"I've been thinking," she said, running her thumb under the brim of her cowboy hat. "If someone like me doesn't take a chance on that mare, she doesn't have much of a future, does she?"

Jessa's eyes shone. She didn't know why she was quite so excited, but it sounded like Mrs. Bailey was going to let Sienna come to Dark Creek.

"I've arranged for the vet and Marjorie to go to the Rescue Society farm on Saturday afternoon."

"The vet?"

"Apparently Sienna is a holy terror to trailer. The vet will sedate her so she travels safely. I've already talked to Dr. Darlington to find out what special care she needs, so we can get her back into reasonable shape as quickly as possible."

"Oh Mrs. Bailey, thank you!" Jessa said, bouncing up and down.

"Don't know why you're thanking me. That horse is going to need a lot of work. And I'm not going to do it all on my own!"

"I'll help!" Jessa said. "I can groom her and maybe start to work with her on the lunge line and. . . ."

"Hold on!" laughed Mrs. Bailey. "Let's get her here first. I have the feeling nothing is going to be easy or quick with this horse."

Each day after school that week, Jessa thought about practising for obedience classes with Romeo.

But each day, something happened which prevented them from getting any serious work done. On Monday and Tuesday, Jessa had to study for a Science test and do spelling corrections. On Wednesday evening, she stayed late at the barn to help get the second stall in the small barn ready for Sienna.

On Thursday, Cheryl invited her over after school and she stayed for dinner. The weather was fantastic on Friday, so she left Romeo in a box stall and headed off on a leisurely trail ride.

When Saturday morning arrived, Romeo was only sitting every other time Jessa asked.

"Some of you have been working very hard, I see," said Rodney Blenkinsop. "Jason—would you like to demonstrate for us?"

A thin young man with short, black hair stepped forward from the group. His gold and white Shetland sheepdog trotted quickly beside him. The dog's eyes never left his owner's face.

"Ask Maestro to sit," Rodney instructed.

Jason stopped and Maestro immediately stopped, looking up expectantly, ears perked forward and his silky tail wagging.

"Sit," Jason said softly. Instantly, the dog sat. His tail never stopped wagging. Now it swept back and forth over the ground.

"Good dog!" Jason said, kneeling beside Maestro to give him a rub behind the ears. Maestro's tail wagged a little faster.

"Excellent!" said Rodney. "How about trying

that with just the hand signal."

Jason and Maestro repeated the exercise perfectly. This time, Jason didn't say a word. He raised his hand and Maestro sat promptly.

Jessa watched, embarrassed. She hoped she wouldn't be called on to demonstrate anything. At her side, Romeo was looking at just about everything except Jessa. With all the distractions, Jessa doubted he would sit on command even once.

"Very good, Jason. Thank you! The exercises you have been doing all week should have helped your dog learn to pay attention to you at all times. You can't teach your dog much if he isn't listening to you."

Jessa tugged at Romeo's leash. He was far more interested in sniffing at Madge, the fluffy black standard poodle beside him than he was in doing what Jessa wanted.

For the rest of the lesson Jessa tried hard to make Romeo sit and lie down. It seemed to her that every other dog was doing better than he was. *This week would be different,* she resolved. They were going to practise every single day, no matter what.

Chapter Seven

Romeo hopped out of the car eagerly when Jessa's mother dropped Jessa and Cheryl off at the barn. He loved Dark Creek and all the delicious smells of chickens and horses.

Jessa knew better than to let him off his leash when she walked up to Mrs. Bailey who was grooming Jasmine in the crossties. As usual, she was crooning a steady stream of endearments to her warmblood chestnut mare.

"Ooh, Jasmine, sweetie. Is Mumsy scratching your special tickly wickly spot?"

Jessa could never quite get used to how much Mrs. Bailey changed whenever she got anywhere near her pride and joy. Normally firm and businesslike, when Mrs. Bailey started fussing over her 1800 pound baby, she turned completely mushy.

Mrs. Bailey massaged a spot on Jasmine's belly just behind her girth. Jasmine groaned with delight and half-closed her eyes.

"Where's Sienna?" Jessa asked.

Mrs. Bailey stopped rubbing and Jasmine opened

her eyes. "They had some trouble loading her. The vet called a little while ago. The trailer should be here any time."

She slipped Jasmine a Fisherman's Friend cough candy, unsnapped the crossties and led Jasmine into her paddock.

"Here they come!" Cheryl shouted when she saw a truck and trailer rolling slowly up the driveway.

The truck stopped and Marjorie hopped out. Her face was set, hard and worried. An ominous thump came from the trailer and it rocked slightly from side to side.

"There's no way to lead her out," she said grimly. "It's best if we just slowly open the door and let her come out on her own. Poor thing. I don't think she's been handled much at all. She should still be slightly sedated. The vet said it would take a couple of hours to wear off completely."

"Stay out of the way, girls," Mrs. Bailey instructed, her voice tight with concern. After loosening the lead shank through the small door by Sienna's head, Mrs. Bailey and Marjorie stood at either side of the back of the trailer. Working together quickly, they let down the ramp and stood back.

None of them was prepared for the horse who bolted backwards down the ramp, her head high and the whites of her eyes showing. If the tranquilizer still ran through her blood, the mare showed no signs of it.

Mrs. Bailey grabbed for the dangling lead line that swung wildly from the mare's halter.

"Barbara! Be careful!" Marjorie cried.

Sienna caught sight of Mrs. Bailey's reaching hand and half-reared. She wheeled away and galloped full tilt down the driveway.

"Did you? . . ." Mrs. Bailey started.

"Yes, yes I shut the gate!" Marjorie finished for her as the mare disappeared around the bend.

A moment later she was back, trotting now, tilting her head up in defiance as she flew past the spectators. Romeo woofed and Jessa told him to sit. To her amazement, he did. But his gaze remained fixed on the mare and not on Jessa.

"How are you going to catch her?" Jessa asked.

"The last thing this mare needs is to be chased around," said Mrs. Bailey gently. "Let's put some fresh hay and water in the paddock by the driveway. Then we'll help her find her way in."

When the paddock was ready for the new occupant, they built a barricade of jump standards and poles across the driveway.

"We can't have her running up and down the driveway all night," muttered Mrs. Bailey. "Besides, you might like to go home sometime."

When the barrier was ready, Mrs. Bailey took up her position perched on the top fence rail beside the gate to the paddock. Jessa locked Romeo in a stall to keep him out of harm's way and then she and Cheryl followed Marjorie to find the mare. Sienna had discovered the tasty grass of Mrs. Bailey's back lawn. She thought nothing of trampling over the flower bed to escape the three humans she saw coming to further torment her.

"Poor girl," Marjorie offered soothingly. Sienna wanted no part of the reassurance and trotted off back down towards the large barn and driveway.

Jessa, Cheryl and Marjorie jogged after her, keeping well back.

By the time Sienna realized her escape route down the driveway had been blocked, the pursuit team had arrived to prevent her running back past the barn. Her only option was to make a break for the gate and into the paddock beyond.

Mrs. Bailey sat as still as stone on the rail beside the open gate. She didn't even look at Sienna. She made a soft, quiet noise in her throat, like a hum or a sigh. Sienna stood stock still, assessing her options. Behind her, Marjorie and the girls stood quietly, their arms outstretched, waiting for the mare's next move.

Jessa hoped the mare didn't charge at her. There was no way she was going to get trampled to death. She'd run so fast in the other direction nobody would be able to catch her.

Beyond Mrs. Bailey, fresh hay and a bucket of grain waited for Sienna. Slowly, the horse began to walk towards the gate, wary of Mrs. Bailey on the fence. Each step she took forward, the girls and Marjorie followed with a step of their own. As the horse drew even with the old woman, Mrs. Bailey quite calmly reached over and yanked the quick release fastener, freeing the dangling lead rope.

Sienna flinched as if her close brush with the

woman's hand had seared her.

Marjorie stepped forward and closed the gate behind the skittish mare.

"Well done, B.B.," she said, using Mrs. Bailey's nickname. Mrs. Bailey climbed down from her perch, coiling the lead rope neatly.

"Couldn't let her run around with this swinging about, now could we?"

Mrs. Bailey studied the mare seriously. "She is going to be difficult. Let's hope we can get her back on her feet again quickly so the Animal Rescue Society can find her a good home. We sure don't have any use for her around here," she added bluntly.

Cheryl and Jessa looked at the little mare eating her hay, never once relaxing. She snatched at the pile and then lifted her head, chewing defiantly as she glared at the girls by the gate.

"She's so thin," said Cheryl. "But her head is pretty. Look how she pricks her ears forward at us."

"What breed is she?" Jessa asked.

"Looks like an old-style Morgan, maybe. Or, maybe she's part draft horse," Marjorie speculated.

"She's a bit small for that," said Mrs. Bailey. "If she had some meat on her bones, she'd be quite stocky. Maybe she's got some quarter horse in her?"

"Look at her fetlocks," said Marjorie pointing at the long feathery hair.

"She sure picked her feet up when she trotted," Cheryl said.

"Actually, it's amazing how well she moved

considering the shape those feet are in!" said Mrs. Bailey.

Sienna's hooves were splayed and cracked and terribly overgrown from lack of care.

"We can't do much to help her if she can't be handled," said Mrs. Bailey. "That's our first priority, then. We have to try and win her trust."

"How are you going to do that?" Cheryl asked. Cheryl ran her hand through her unruly shock of red hair. No matter how short she kept it, her hair always looked a bit of a mess.

"When she gets used to the idea we are the source of good food, that will be a start. We'll give her a few days to settle in, and to let her realize she's safe here."

A baleful wail rose from the barn. The girls left the mare to eat in peace.

"So, how come Romeo has to spend his life in jail?" Cheryl asked.

Romeo's nose, flanked by two white paws, peeped over the top of the stall door. His paws barely reached the top of the door.

"Just until he learns to behave himself. Which reminds me, I should practise."

Jessa opened the door and snapped on his leash. He was so excited to be freed from imprisonment he leaped and danced in circles until both he and Jessa were completely entangled.

Cheryl's giggles turned into a full-scale belly laugh.

"Oh, you two are good!" she mocked.

"I'd like to see you do better," Jessa replied, stepping out of the web made by dog and leash as gracefully as she could manage.

"Sit!" she commanded. Romeo wagged his tail and looked up at her.

"Impressive," smirked Cheryl.

Jessa trotted backwards to the end of the leash. "Romeo come!"

Romeo sat. Jessa wiggled the leash. The dog didn't budge. His head tipped from side to side as he watched Jessa get more and more agitated. She slapped her thigh with her hand, trying to encourage her dog to move. Romeo acted as if he had no idea what she wanted. He lay down and put his chin on his paws. When Jessa tried to make him get up by pulling on his collar, he rolled on his back and waved his paws in the air.

"Romeo!" she sputtered. "Cut it out!"

"That looks like fun," Cheryl said. "I think I should take Ginger to classes."

Jessa gave up. She plunked herself on the ground and scratched Romeo's tummy. His eyes closed and his tongue lolled out between his gleaming white teeth.

"Ginger could use a refresher course."

Refresher course? It seemed to Jessa that Ginger, the Waters' dog, was already perfect. She could already sit, come, stay and roll over.

"We could have so much fun in the same class, don't you think? I'll ask my mom if we can join. It doesn't look like we've missed much."

Jessa didn't say anything. Part of her wanted Cheryl and Ginger to join the classes—it would be more fun if she knew someone. But another part of her didn't want Cheryl around to watch her struggles with Romeo. Maybe Cheryl would have changed her mind by the following Saturday.

Whether Cheryl and her wonder dog came to class or not, Jessa vowed silently to make up for lost time and work at her dog training every single day.

Chapter Eight

All week Jessa struggled with Romeo. By Wednesday, he was pretty good at sitting. On her way home from school she decided to teach him how to lie down on command. She wouldn't leave for the barn until he had done it perfectly three times. *Nothing would stop her,* she decided grimly as she walked in the back door.

"Hold it right there, Jessa Marie Richardson."

Jessa stopped half way across the kitchen. Her mother only ever called her by her full name when Jessa was in trouble.

"What did I do?"

"That dog has to go."

"Why? What did he do?"

Jessa's mother pointed towards the dining room door. Jessa's stomach lurched when she stepped through the door. The carpet was covered with dirt and every single one of her mother's precious houseplants lay wilted and torn on the floor.

"Do you think any of them are poisonous?" Jessa asked, suddenly worried that Romeo might have consumed something toxic.

"Poisonous? That dog deserves to be poisoned if you ask me." Jessa's mother was furious. "He even knocked over my favourite palm tree in the living room!"

Jessa's mother looked to be on the verge of tears. How anyone could be so attached to a bunch of plants was beyond Jessa.

"I'll clean it all up—don't worry," she said. "Where's the dog?"

"I locked him in your room. You'd better check on him, I suppose. When you've taken him out for a quick walk, feed him up there and come help clean this up. I'll get started. Maybe some of the stronger plants can be saved."

With a plan of action, her mother seemed calmer. The heaviness in her voice made Jessa wish she could somehow press 'rewind' and erase all the damage her dog had done. Even Romeo's wagging tail did little to lift her spirits. She knew it would take more than vacuuming the spilled potting soil to restore her mother's good humour.

Cleaning up after the plant disaster took forever. The dirt had scattered absolutely everywhere. She and her mother worked quietly, not chatting like they usually did. Jessa rushed through her dinner, finished her homework and then headed out into the backyard to work with Romeo. By now, Romeo realized that the leash and the backyard meant work. For a change, he was rather cooperative.

"Mom, could we maybe build Romeo a run outside so he can have somewhere safe to stay when I'm at school?"

"Don't talk like that, Jessa. I'm going to call all the vets and the radio station again tomorrow. I'm sure someone is going to claim him. For now, he can wait for you in your bedroom. Just pick up anything you don't want eaten."

Jessa sighed. "What happens if nobody claims him? We've had him for nearly three weeks already."

"I've been thinking about that. I think we should put up a poster at the pet store and try to find him a good home."

"But. . . ."

"These obedience classes won't do him any harm. But really, Jessa, you can see we aren't organized to have a dog."

"If he had a doghouse and a run. . . ."

"Jessa. That's enough. Are you still going to the barn tonight?"

"Yes," Jessa answered sullenly. At least Rebel wouldn't argue with her. Romeo put his chin on Jessa's knee and looked up at her. She patted his head and blinked, determined not to cry. There had to be a way to convince her mother that they needed a dog. And not just any dog. Romeo. It wasn't his fault nobody had ever taken the time to teach him how to behave.

"Whoa!" Mrs. Bailey walked slowly across the paddock towards Sienna. The grain swished tantalizingly in the bottom of the pail she held out in front of her. Jessa hung over the top rail of the fence, watching. The mare glared at Mrs. Bailey and began to back up. Mrs. Bailey hadn't even made it half way across the paddock when Sienna wheeled around and cantered to the farthest corner. Mrs. Bailey stopped and put the bucket on the ground. With her hands on her hips she looked perplexed.

"She's so stubborn," she said. "I've never met a horse who couldn't be bribed before."

Slowly, Mrs. Bailey backed away. It wasn't until she had slipped through the gate that the little horse made her way to the bucket and consumed the grain.

"The stronger she gets, the more determined she is to stay away. I don't quite know what to do with her. Marjorie gave me the name of a fellow who has quite a reputation for working with difficult horses. I think maybe I'll give him a call to see if he can help. I feel obliged to keep trying, you know?"

Jessa knew how Mrs. Bailey felt. It didn't seem right to give up on the mare because she had been treated badly in the past. And yet, watching her gobbling down her grain, ready to flee at the slightest excuse, Jessa couldn't imagine how anyone was going to get close enough to gentle her. Jessa's idea of grooming and getting Sienna used to human contact seemed ludicrous when there was no way to get anywhere near her, never mind tie her up.

Jessa had arrived at the barn too late to ride, but that didn't stop her from leading Rebel out of his stall and giving him a thorough going over. He had obviously rolled during the day and dirt rose from his back as she whisked away with a dandy brush. She hummed to herself as she worked. Romeo lay quietly where she had tied him up. He watched her vigorous currying, craning his head to keep her in sight when she moved around to Rebel's other side.

Rebel seemed only mildly curious about the newcomer. He was far more interested in trying to determine which of Jessa's pockets contained the carrot pieces.

When Jessa looked at the dog again a few minutes later, he had his head in her grooming caddy.

"Romeo! Get out of there!"

Romeo lifted his head innocently. He was chewing on a sponge.

"Hey! Give that back!"

Jessa pried the sponge from between the dog's teeth and moved the caddy out of his reach. "Brat!" she said, giving him a playful swat on the behind.

In the cool breeze of early evening as she brushed out Rebel's mane, Jessa realized there was no place she would rather be, nothing else she would rather be doing. She knelt down and gave her pesky dog a scratch behind the ear. She wasn't quite sure how she was going to manage, but one way or the other, she was determined to keep Romeo. Romeo gave the back of her hand a little lick and sighed contentedly. If there was one thing she had learned from her resourceful and independent mother: if you wanted something badly enough, there was usually a way to make it happen.

Chapter Nine

"What's going on?" Jessa asked as she walked into the riding ring. Mrs. Bailey put down the sledgehammer and straightened up.

"Walter Walters, this is Jessa. She's the girl who rides the little bay pony, Rebel."

A man wearing a knitted woolen hat grinned at her. *It was hardly the season for woolen caps*, Jessa thought. With his yellow suspenders, plaid shirt and grey whiskers he looked like a lumberjack from the pictures in her Social Studies textbook.

Nails bristled from between his teeth but he managed to say a friendly 'howdy'. He took one of the nails from his mouth and pounded it through a piece of plywood into a fence post. Jessa stared at the strange construction.

"What are you making?"

"A round pen," Mrs. Bailey said, puffing slightly. "Can you pound this in?"

Jessa took the sledgehammer. It felt like it weighed more than she did. She climbed up on the mounting block where Mrs. Bailey had been standing and dropped the sledgehammer onto the top of the fence post. It didn't seem to move at all.

"You'll have to pound harder than that or we'll be here all year," Mrs. Bailey said.

Jessa tried again. She tried to swing the sledge-hammer harder. The stubby head thunked against the top of the post.

"That's better. Again."

Jessa swung harder. She felt like she was going to fall off the mounting block. Over and over she lifted the heavy sledgehammer and let it fall onto the post. Finally, Mrs. Bailey told her to stop and they traded places. Mrs. Bailey gave a couple of mighty swings and then stepped back to look at their work.

"That'll do," she said and moved onto the next post. "Thank goodness we're pounding these into hogsfuel and sand! We'd never manage otherwise."

In all, there were about twenty posts in a circle in the middle of the riding ring. To make the pen have solid sides, Walter Walters was busy hammering sheets of plywood to the posts.

"What's this for?" Jessa asked.

"Walter wants to try something with Sienna."

"Why doesn't he just use the riding ring?" Jessa asked.

"Too big," grunted Mrs. Bailey, hefting the sledgehammer and letting it fall on the next post. "We're nearly done. We've been at this for hours. Here." She handed Jessa the sledgehammer. "You're young and strong. Give that a few whacks."

Jessa struggled with the sledgehammer. *Surely*

there had to be a machine that could pound in fence posts. Doing it by hand was crazy.

Crazy or not, the three of them managed to finish the round pen. With his mouth emptied of nails, Walter could speak quite normally.

"That's a nice little pony you have there," he said. "Real nice."

Walter's voice was gentle, soft. He had a very faint accent that made his words go up and down like a kind of song.

"What are you going to do with Sienna?" she wanted to know. It didn't seem fair that such a frightened horse should be trapped in a relatively small pen where she couldn't even run away.

Walter took his cap off and scratched his head. "What do you think is wrong with her?" he asked.

Jessa wasn't sure what he was getting at. "She's still pretty thin."

"No, I don't mean her health. Why do you think she acts so wild?"

"I think she's scared."

Walter nodded. "Why?"

"Ummm, I guess because somebody beat her."

"Would that make her act wild?"

"I guess so. I think she's scared. But maybe she's also acting tough, like she doesn't need to have friends."

"In the wild, do mustangs like to be alone?"

Jessa thought of her poster of wild mustangs that hung over her desk. The herd was beautiful, about thirty horses in full gallop, plunging into a creek.

"No. They live in herds."

"Right. So I think that little mare would be happier if she felt like she belonged to someone. Someone who could look after her, protect her."

"But how?" Jessa was mystified.

"We have to make her believe it's better to trust us than to fight or run away."

Jessa looked at the skinny little old man and his baggy work pants held up with suspenders and then at the makeshift round pen he had built with Mrs. Bailey. If Mrs. Bailey hadn't managed to get within six metres of the mare even armed with a bucket of grain, she couldn't imagine what this old guy was going to do to convince Sienna it was worth it to be his friend.

Between the opening to the round pen and Sienna's paddock, Mrs. Bailey and Walter had made a chute by using jump standards, poles, and stacked up hay bales. Once the gate to her paddock was opened, Sienna really had no choice but to follow the crude passageway all the way into the round pen.

"Ready, Barbara?" Walter asked.

"Ready. I'll go open the gate."

"Watch yourself," Walter said. "She may kick out, or try to wheel around. Just be ready for anything."

The three of them watched Sienna wind her way along the makeshift path to the round pen. She stepped inside the odd-looking structure with a snort. Behind her, Walter slid three rails into place. Sienna was trapped. She moved warily to the far side of the pen.

The walls were high enough she couldn't see out, except for the gate made of the three rails. Mrs. Bailey threw two heavy winter horse blankets over the rails so it was more difficult for Sienna to see out.

When Walter stepped into the pen with the half-wild mare, Jessa fully expected to see him trampled into the dust. She and Mrs. Bailey stood on a hay bale so they could see into the pen more easily.

Walter pulled a piece of heavy string from his back pocket. Sienna's nostrils flared. Very casually, Walter tossed the cord in Sienna's general direction, holding onto one end. She took off running, her head and tail high. She tore around the inside of the pen. Jessa's heart raced, watching the mare trying to escape. Walter gently flicked the cord at her again, and Sienna ran on.

"I'll just keep her moving for a few minutes. Horses will run a certain distance before they want to stop naturally. You can see the cord isn't touching her, or hurting her in any way."

Even though the piece of string was harmless, Sienna sped up a little each time Walter cast it towards her. It wasn't long before she was looking a little tired, like she wanted to stop and rest.

"She's not in great shape, so it didn't take her long to start looking at me like that. . . . See what her ear is doing?"

Jessa watched the horse's ear that was closest to Walter. It was no longer pricked forward. It was cocked toward the wiry little man in the middle of the pen. Sienna was really slowing down now. She looked pretty tired already. Walter threw the line towards her again, encouraging her to keep moving.

"Watch her head start to drop now," he instructed. Sure enough, the horse's head moved closer to the ground. "Ah, she's chewing—look you can see her tongue."

It was true. Sienna was no longer tearing around the pen looking for an escape route. She was concentrating on Walter. Her head dropped lower and her lower jaw chewed. Her tongue licked in and out of her mouth.

"Let's see what happens here," Walter said softly and turned away from the mare. He stood very still, his eyes looking at the ground in front of him, his shoulders turned away from the horse.

Sienna stopped. What happened next was incredible. Very slowly, she walked up behind Walter. Walter didn't look up. He seemed to sense her presence. He moved away and she followed, her nose just touching his elbow.

Jessa could hardly breathe. All the fine hair on her arms stood straight up. *What was going on?* For the whole time Sienna had been at Dark Creek, she never been that close to anybody!

Very slowly, Walter turned around. Sienna took a step backwards and Walter cast the line again. Once more, the little horse ran to the edge of the round pen. This time, it was only a few minutes before her head dropped and she started the funny chewing motion again. Once more, Walter dropped his arms to his sides and turned away. And, once again, Sienna came into the middle of the pen to be near him. Like a big dog, she turned when he turned and followed him as he zigzagged around. He stopped. Sienna stopped. Walter quietly turned to face her and, moving very slowly, he reached up and rubbed her on the forehead between the eyes. He murmured something softly.

Jessa fully expected the mare to race off again. But she didn't. Instead, she stood very still, almost as if relieved to be able to stay in the middle of the pen with this total stranger.

Jessa felt Mrs. Bailey's hand reach over and squeeze her on the shoulder. She looked up and was surprised to see Mrs. Bailey's eyes were moist. "I do believe that little mare is going to be okay," said Mrs. Bailey.

Jessa nodded. She didn't trust herself to speak. In the round pen, Walter was very quietly stroking the mare's neck and shoulder. She just stood there, waiting to see what he was going to do next.

What he did was snap a lead shank on her halter. Leaving lots of slack, he turned and walked away from her. She followed.

"Go ahead and take down the rails," Walter said. "Nice and easy."

While Mrs. Bailey and Jessa quickly and quietly removed the rails, Walter led Sienna all the way back down the chute to her paddock. The structure seemed completely unnecessary now. Sienna looked like she would have followed Walter Walters to the end of the earth.

Chapter Ten

"It was like he put a spell on her or something," Jessa said, trying to explain to Cheryl how Walter had handled Sienna.

"And then he just led her back to the paddock?" Cheryl sounded unconvinced.

"It was amazing," Jessa said. "She let him touch her. He's going to be there again after school. Do you want to come with me?"

"Absolutely!" Cheryl said.

Jessa and Cheryl raced home after school, freed Romeo from Jessa's room and jogged down to the barn. The chute had been dismantled. Walter had Sienna in the round pen again. This time, he had a bucket filled with brushes in the middle of the pen. It only took a couple of minutes with the light line and Sienna was giving him that same look which said, 'I want to come into the middle and be with you'.

Jessa whispered to Cheryl what was going on.

"Now he's going to turn away, see? And she's going to start to come into the middle. . . ."

Sure enough, the mare was soon right behind Walter. He turned around and gently rubbed her between the eyes. Then he ran his hands down her neck, over her back and down her legs. As he touched each new place, she flinched a little, but she didn't bolt. As he worked with her, she relaxed, allowing him to rub her withers and back, even to reach under her belly and stroke her there.

Walter talked softly to her, a steady murmur of comforting sounds. He told her what he was going to do, and then very quietly, he did it. After he had used his hands, he repeated the whole process with a soft brush.

At the end of the session, he led her back to her paddock and turned her out. She walked over to her fresh hay and began to eat.

"That's not the same horse," said Cheryl, her voice filled with admiration.

Walter smiled. "Mrs. Bailey wants me to go real slow. It won't be long before we can get her used to a saddle."

Jessa's eyes nearly popped out of her head. "A saddle? Isn't that a bit dangerous?"

"I'm an old guy," laughed Walter. "I don't do anything too dangerous."

"I don't know about that," Mrs. Bailey said. "You did agree to let me cook dinner for you."

Cheryl's eyebrows shot up. Mrs. Bailey was not exactly famous for her cooking skills.

Jessa dug her elbow into her friend's side, but not before Mrs. Bailey saw Cheryl's look of horror.

"Don't worry, Cheryl. I need him back to work with this mare. I'm not going to poison him."

"Let's go work with Romeo before we get Rebel out," said Jessa quickly, trying to rescue her friend.

But Cheryl didn't seem too keen to be rescued. "If Mr. Walters can survive being in a pen with a wild horse, I'm sure he'll be fine in your kitchen."

Jessa yanked on Cheryl's arm and pulled her towards the barn. "Come on," she said. Mrs. Bailey wasn't the type to tolerate cheeky remarks from kids. But Mrs. Bailey had already turned back to Walter. They were talking about the schedule for the rest of the week.

"I'll see if Tony Frey can come to trim those feet in the next day or so. And on Saturday, I'll ask Dr. Darlington to have a look at her. That cut over her eye is still a bit swollen."

Walter nodded and the two of them walked off together, chatting about Sienna and the best way to proceed with her training.

Jessa marched briskly behind Jason and Maestro.

"Halt!" said Rodney.

Maestro's neck seemed permanently turned so he could watch Jason's every move. Jason's left hand hung loosely by his side, the leash swinging gently in front of him. He talked continuously to his dog, kind words of encouragement as they made crisp, precise turns at each corner.

"Ouch!" Jessa muttered as Romeo yelped and jumped sideways out of her way when they tried to make a left turn.

"Good one, Jessa," Cheryl quipped from behind her.

Jessa rolled her eyes. Of course Cheryl would have to see every little mistake.

"Ooof! Sorry!"

Jessa had been so busy worrying about what Cheryl might be seeing that she hadn't noticed when Rodney called out, "Halt!"

"I'm so sorry."

"No problem," said Jason, despite the fact Jessa had just crashed into him from behind. Maestro stayed sitting quietly at Jason's side. He didn't even move when Romeo pawed at him playfully.

Jessa dragged her dog backwards and made him sit at her side. She was still trying to organize the leash when she heard, "Forward!"

Off they went again.

"Jessa, don't let him bite the leash like that!"

Jessa jerked the leash away. Romeo barked and Rodney gave them an exasperated look.

"Good, Cheryl!" he said, turning his attention to Cheryl and Ginger. "Everyone, prepare to reverse directions. . . . And, reverse!"

Jessa stumbled over Romeo and he scuttled sideways to get out of her way.

"Jessa!" said Rodney. "Which way are you supposed to turn when you do an about-face?"

"To the right," Jessa answered miserably, the colour rising in her cheeks.

"And why do you turn to the right?"

"So the dog goes around me. . . ."

". . . and you don't fall over the dog."

Jessa's blush deepened. She knew she was supposed to do her U-turns to the right. The trouble was she had far too much to think about! It wasn't easy to give the right commands, hold the leash properly, and remember to praise Romeo when he managed to do something right.

She kept walking, now close on Cheryl's heels. Ginger trotted smartly at her friend's side, her tail wagging back and forth with each bouncy step.

"Halt!"

Jessa stopped and pulled on Romeo who actually sat, though his back end poked out sideways at a very strange angle.

"That's a nice straight sit, Ginger and Cheryl!"

Cheryl swivelled around and beamed at Jessa. "Isn't this fun?"

"Yeah. A ton of fun."

"Before you all leave today, I have an announcement to make." Rodney looked very pleased with himself. Most of the dogs were already showing great improvement in their manners.

Jessa and Cheryl squatted down beside their dogs. Romeo took advantage of the quiet moment to roll over on his back. Jessa scratched his belly and listened.

"Dog training should be fun!" Rodney began, rubbing his hands together.

Jessa was beginning to doubt that 'fun' had anything to do with obedience training.

"By the end of this course, your dog should be able to sit, stay, lie down and come on command. They should also walk politely at your left side. Some of you will even be doing the heeling exercise without a leash."

Jessa had heard his promises before. Given the meager progress she and Romeo had made after three weeks of lessons, she doubted they would graduate.

Cheryl and Jason exchanged a look that clearly said they were both planning to be among those who mastered leash-less heeling.

"We'll also have a Top Dog Award for the dog who performs the most amazing trick on graduation day. If you want ideas or tips on how to teach your old dogs new tricks, come and see me."

"Cool!" squealed Cheryl. "I have a great idea for a trick! Everyone will love it!"

Inwardly, Jessa groaned. She looked at Romeo sprawled on his back and wondered what kind of amazing trick she could possibly teach him.

"Are you coming to the barn?" Jessa asked at the end of class.

"No. I'm getting my haircut. Maybe tomorrow."

"Sure. Maybe."

Jessa wasn't that disappointed her friend was busy. She was getting just a little annoyed with Cheryl and the way she always liked to be centre stage. *Why couldn't she just blend into the crowd sometimes?*

Chapter Eleven

"Jessa! We were just talking about you," said Walter as Jessa joined Mrs. Bailey outside the round pen.

Sienna stood quietly beside Walter. The good hay and gentle handling seemed to agree with the little mare. Her hip bones weren't sticking out so much. Now that Walter could actually catch and handle her, the farrier had been able to trim her neglected feet. The vet was scheduled for a visit later in the day.

"Do you want to come in here with me?" Walter asked.

"Me?" Jessa looked over her shoulder. "You want me to come in there?"

"Sure. Come on."

"Here, I'll hold that dog of yours," said Mrs. Bailey, taking Romeo's leash.

Jessa's heart thumped as she slipped under the bottom rail and stood inside the pen.

"Come on over here, nice and slow," said Walter.

Sienna watched her, ever vigilant, a little less

certain of herself now that someone new was in the pen.

"That's it, Jessa, just move slow and easy. Come right beside me."

Slowly, Jessa extended the back of her hand towards Sienna. The mare stretched her head forward and sniffed at the newcomer. She snorted and Jessa felt Sienna's warm, moist breath on the back of her hand.

She laughed and Sienna jerked back, startled.

"Steady there, girl. There's a good girl," murmured Walter, calmly stroking the mare's neck.

"Take a little step forward there, Jessa. That's it. Now, nice and easy, but confident like, reach up and rub her between the eyes."

Jessa held her breath.

"Relax, Jessa. She can feel all that tension of yours. Think real soft, gentle thoughts, tell her you ain't going to hurt her. Horses can tell what you're thinking, you know."

"It's okay, girl," Jessa said softly. "It's okay. I'm just going to rub your head, just like this."

Jessa's fingers touched the mare's forehead. Sienna stood motionless, intent and cautious, just like Jessa.

"That's it, Jessa. Move slowly round her so you can reach her neck. That's a girl. A little firmer, let her feel your confidence. There, now, can you feel her relaxing?"

Jessa concentrated on Walter's soothing voice. She felt Sienna relax beneath her hands. Slowly and methodically, she worked her way over the horse's back, smoothing and stroking, easing away both Sienna's fears and her own.

"Good girl, Sienna," she whispered, and Sienna's ear flicked back to catch the soft sound. "Good, good girl," Jessa said. She glanced over at Mrs. Bailey. The older woman nodded and flashed her a rare, wide grin. Mrs. Bailey gave Jessa a thumbs up sign and nodded again.

Jessa had no idea that simply touching a horse could be such an extraordinary experience. She felt nearly overwhelmed with a feeling of tender protectiveness. *What must it take*, she wondered, *for a horse who had been so badly abused, to allow herself to trust again?*

Jessa stayed in the pen with Walter long enough to groom Sienna and pick out her feet. Walter seemed to have all the patience in the world as Jessa slowly gained confidence as she worked with the shy horse.

"Soon," Walter said. "Soon we'll try that saddle."

Dr. Darlington arrived shortly after the end of the training session.

"Let's have a look at that eye," she said.

Walter stood at Sienna's head, keeping her quiet while the vet inspected the cut.

"It's actually healing quite well on its own," she said after she had cleaned the wound thoroughly. "I'll leave some of this ointment here. Put it on twice a day and call me if it starts to swell up or if there's a discharge. Otherwise, she's looking a whole lot better than the first time I saw her. You're doing a fine job. You know, she's actually quite a pretty mare."

"What kind of horse do you think she is?" Jessa asked.

Dr. Darlington stood back and had a long, hard look. "Hard to say. She might have some Morgan in her."

"That's what Marjorie said," Jessa said, though she couldn't see much resemblance between Marjorie's elegant mare, Babe, and the scruffy horse in front of her.

"Well, if she's registered, she may have a chip," the vet suggested. "I can check for you."

"A chip?" Jessa asked, following the vet to her truck. "What's a chip?"

"A microchip. You don't see nearly as many tattoos these days. Microchips are the modern way of identifying animals—dogs, cats, parrots—they can all be marked that way. Yesterday, I even implanted chips in some ostriches!"

Jessa was mystified. She looked back at Sienna. "Can't you just see the chip?" she asked. "How big is it? How do you fasten them on?"

Dr. Darlington smiled. She fished out a small rectangular box that looked like a cross between a TV remote control and a calculator.

"The chips are about the size of a grain of rice. They're implanted under the skin."

The vet scanned the little device over Sienna's

neck. About half way between her withers and her poll, the machine beeped twice.

"Well, what do you know! She's a registered something! Here's her number."

A number appeared in the little glowing screen. Dr. Darlington wrote it down.

"I'll call the animal registry and find out what I can. We should hear back in a few days."

"Well I'll be jiggered," Walter said, scratching the back of his neck. "What will they think of next?"

Grooming Rebel a little later took on a whole new significance. Jessa no longer took for granted his gentle, playful nature. Just as she had with Sienna, she ran her hands along his neck, under his belly, down his legs. She had never appreciated his calm acceptance of her touch and the trust that implied.

She threw her arms around her pony's neck and buried her face in his mane. He nuzzled her back, gently lipping her hair.

Tied nearby, Romeo whined.

"Don't get jealous," Jessa said, going to him and giving his head a rub. His tail thumped happily on the ground. Now, if only she could think of a good trick to teach him . . . though she would settle for him coming when he was called!

Chapter Twelve

Romeo chased Ginger around Jessa's backyard. "Go Ginger!" Cheryl shouted, cheering her dog on. Romeo was bigger but Ginger was a little speed demon! When the dogs had worn themselves out, the girls snapped on the leashes and headed out the back gate and into the alley.

They took turns calling out commands. "Halt!" "Reverse direction!" "Make your dog lie down!"

"Romeo's doing pretty well," said Cheryl. It was true. Jessa had to agree that her extra work with the dog was starting to pay off. His sits were still very crooked and pretty slow compared to Ginger's, but he was a lot better than when they had started.

"Watch this!" said Cheryl. She pointed her finger at Ginger and said, "Bang!!"

Ginger staggered two steps sideways and collapsed. She lay motionless on her side, her eyes closed.

"Pretty good, hunh?"

"Yeah, not bad," Jessa agreed.

"She'll stay like that until she hears a certain word."

"What kind of a word?" Jessa wondered. *What would happen if Cheryl suddenly dropped dead—did anyone else know the secret word that would allow Ginger to get up again?*

"She was in a play once and she was trained to play dead until a certain line in the play. The word which gets her up again is 'resurrection'."

When Ginger heard the word 'resurrection', she jumped up and ran to Cheryl who gave her a huge hug and a big kiss on the forehead. Jessa watched glumly. *How on earth was she supposed to teach Romeo a trick that could beat a performance like that?*

"Yes, yes, I understand." Mrs. Bailey was on the tack room phone when Jessa and Cheryl arrived at the barn with their dogs. Jessa loved the fact her little house on Desdemona Street was close enough to the barn that she could walk there in only fifteen minutes.

"I'm sorry, but there's no way I'm going to push her along too quickly," Mrs. Bailey said. When she hung up, her face was flushed. "Well, seems like a family has come forward to adopt Sienna."

A sick feeling squeezed Jessa's stomach.

"Which, of course, is wonderful news. We knew she would be leaving again. But it's too early to let her go quite yet. Why, we've only just started to work on her stable manners! No, letting her go before she's ready might set her way back."

It sounded to Jessa that Mrs. Bailey was trying to

convince herself of something.

Jessa and Cheryl took some carrots out to Sienna. The mare recognized Jessa and when she saw the gift of carrots, she came straight over to the fence. She took the carrots the girls offered and then retreated once again to the far side of her paddock. Her short tail swished at the flies buzzing around her.

After hours of trying to work through the matted clumps filled with burrs, Mrs. Bailey and Jessa had finally resorted to cutting out the thickest clumps. All that was left was a short, straggly tail that at least was composed only of horsehair.

"She's so much better," Cheryl remarked.

Jessa couldn't answer. Sienna watched her from the far side of the paddock. They looked at each other for a long time, saying nothing but sharing a quiet calm. Jessa knew she should be happy that a potential home had been found for Sienna, but instead she felt only a vague sadness, a sense of impending loss.

The moment was shattered when Walter Walter's old truck crunched its way up the gravel driveway. The girls caught Rebel and led him up to the barn. They could hear Mrs. Bailey and Walter talking in the tack room.

Mrs. Bailey was chuckling and then Walter let out a bellow. Jessa wondered what joke they were sharing. Still laughing, they emerged into the sunlight as Jessa snapped Rebel into the crossties.

"Hello there, Jessa," Walter smiled. "Ready to do

some more work with our friend?"

"Oh, yes please," Jessa grinned.

"I'm going to give Walter a cup of tea up at the house," said Mrs. Bailey. "We'll meet you down here a little later this afternoon."

Mrs. Bailey and Walter strolled off to the house together.

"Ooooh," said Cheryl.

"What do you mean, 'ooooh'?" Jessa asked.

"Look how close together they're walking."

Jessa watched the retreating pair. "So? They're old. They have to walk close together or they can't hear each other."

"No way," said Cheryl. "Can't you tell? They *like* each other."

"Oh don't be ridiculous!" Jessa snorted. "They're way too old for that! Walter happens to be great with horses. Mrs. Bailey is just being nice because she's grateful for all his help. That's all."

"Yeah, right, Jessa. My highly attuned powers of intuition tell me those two *like* each other. And I don't mean just as horse people."

Jessa tacked up Rebel and left Cheryl to dog-sit. Walter insisted horses could tell exactly what their riders were thinking. Jessa decided to experiment with Rebel.

Once Rebel had settled into a nice, even trot, Jessa started thinking about every aid before she actually gave it. It seemed like Rebel responded more quickly than usual. Of course, Jessa reasoned, that might have been because she was better prepared to ask for a lead change because she had thought all the steps through ahead of time.

That theory didn't explain Rebel's reactions to the non-existent snakes, though. Once, approaching the far corner, Jessa imagined a whole nest of snakes lying in wait. When Rebel drew close to that corner, he sped up and veered away, almost as if he had really seen the twisting mass of snakes in Jessa's head.

Immediately, she felt guilty and pulled him up. "Sorry, Rebel," she said and rubbed his neck. The next time they rode past the scary corner, Jessa was careful to think only of grass. Rebel soon settled down again.

Jessa decided not to experiment any more. It was a bit creepy to think horses might actually be able to read minds.

After her ride, Cheryl and Jessa rubbed Rebel down and led him back out to his paddock. Mrs. Bailey and Walter joined them at Sienna's gate a few minutes later. Jessa watched the two grown-ups carefully but she could see no evidence that they were anything other than two concerned horse people.

Cheryl seemed to think otherwise. When Mrs. Bailey opened the gate for Walter, Cheryl nudged Jessa in the ribs and jiggled her eyebrows up and down.

Jessa nudged her back and scowled. *Cheryl's imagination was really working overtime today!*

"So, you ready?" Walter asked. Jessa nodded. She was looking forward to working with Sienna in the round pen.

Tossing the light line towards the mare, she sent Sienna off, running around the pen. After only a few minutes, the mare asked to come into the middle of the pen to join Jessa.

Working slowly, with Jessa holding the mare's lead shank, Walter began to get the horse used to the saddle pad and saddle. Jessa was amazed at how calmly Sienna accepted first the pad and then the saddle and finally, even the girth.

As Walter slowly tightened the girth, Jessa talked soothingly to Sienna who paid close attention to the equipment being strapped to her back.

Without stirrup leathers, and with the saddle securely on her back, Walter sent Sienna around the pen again. She didn't try to buck or kick, though she did flick her ears back and forth as she caught the faint, unfamiliar sounds of the leather squeaking.

"Steady now," Walter soothed.

"Good girl, Sienna," Jessa praised.

Sienna came back into the center of the pen when Walter turned away. Both Jessa and Walter fussed over her. Jessa slipped her a piece of carrot from her pocket and Sienna nudged her in return.

"Let's try something," Walter suggested. "Come here."

He smacked the saddle lightly. Sienna flinched and Jessa froze. *Now what was he doing?*

Methodically, Walter worked over the saddle. He slapped it louder and harder, lifted the flaps, tugged on the billets and wiggled the saddle from side to side. Gradually, Sienna relaxed until she hardly seemed bothered at all by Walter's antics.

Jessa slipped her another carrot. Sienna deserved a reward for putting up with all this nonsense.

"Jessa," Walter asked. "Is a horse a predator?"

"No."

"No, of course not. A horse is prey. What can a wild horse do if it gets attacked by a wolf or a mountain lion?"

"Run away?"

"Exactly. That's what a horse wants to do when it feels threatened."

Jessa reached out to gently touch Sienna's neck.

"What do you think a horse thinks when we put on a saddle? Or, when a rider climbs up on her back?"

Jessa didn't say anything. She wasn't quite sure what Walter was getting at.

"A predator might jump onto a horse's back, right? So, what could a horse do about that?"

"Buck and kick and try to run away?"

"Exactly. So, we have to get her used to the idea that even with something stuck on her back, she's still safe here with us."

Jessa kept scratching Sienna's neck while Walter repeated his fiddling with the straps and flaps on the other side of the saddle.

"Okay, you ready?"

"Ready for what?" Jessa asked dubiously.

"Here, give me the lead shank and I'll give you a boost."

"A boost? But—I don't think I'm ready to ride her. . . ." Jessa said nervously.

Chapter Thirteen

"Calm down. She's not ready for you either. I just want you to flop over the saddle—on your belly. Just be ready to jump back down if she panics. She won't. At first, just stay very, very still so she can get used to the whole idea of having something alive and warm on her back."

After their little discussion about horses bucking and fleeing in order to dislodge a predator, Jessa wasn't exactly happy about what she was being asked to do.

From outside the pen, Mrs. Bailey gave her a smile of encouragement. Cheryl's eyes looked about ready to pop out of her head!

"Are you sure?" Jessa asked.

"Sure as I'm standing here in front of you. Just make sure you think real, nice thoughts, okay?"

Jessa swallowed guiltily. Walter seemed to have an uncanny ability to know what a horse was thinking. She wondered if he was able to read human minds, too, whether he had guessed the snake trick she had played on Rebel.

She took a deep breath and Walter helped her lie across Sienna's back. The saddle pressed into her tummy.

Sienna tensed and Jessa could almost feel her thinking about running off. Jessa closed her eyes and concentrated on her breathing—slow and steady—in and out. She conjured up an image of a wide-open prairie, grasses nodding gently in the breeze under a white-hot sun.

"Jessa?"

Jessa left the sun-drenched prairie landscape in her head and pulled herself back into the round pen.

"I said to hop off."

Jessa pushed herself backwards, off the mare and away from the saddle. Sienna took a step in the other direction but stopped when she felt Walter's reassuring hand on her neck.

Jessa gazed into Sienna's eyes, sharing a silent 'thank you'. The wildness and fear had gone from the mare's look. It had been replaced by a wary intelligence, a look that said, 'I trust you for as long as you deserve to be trusted. Betray me, and. . . .'

"Ready to try that again?"

For the next fifteen minutes Jessa flopped on and off Sienna's back like a warm sack of potatoes. Before long, Walter was leading them around and Jessa was wiggling in place, her arms and legs flopping loosely as they worked together to get the mare used to movement against her sides.

Jessa didn't much like 'riding' with her head hanging down. It did weird things to her balance.

Before advancing to each new challenge, they waited until Sienna was quiet, calm and accepting.

"Not a bad session," Walter remarked when Sienna was tied at the barn for a good grooming. "Just about time somebody rode her, don't you think?"

Jessa beamed. She couldn't believe her luck. If anyone had told her she would actually be riding the mare everyone had thought was untamable, she would have thought them crazy.

The phone in the tack room rang shrilly and Mrs. Bailey ran to answer it.

"Well isn't that interesting," she said so loudly she could be clearly heard outside. "Thank you so much for calling."

She hung up the phone and joined the others. "Sienna is a purebred, registered Canadian Horse."

"Well, I'll be jiggered," said Walter. "That's one of Canada's oldest breeds! I should have known. My grandfather had a beautiful pair of black Canadians. They were so tough, those little horses, they called them 'Little Iron Horses'. There aren't many around these days."

"That's right," said Mrs. Bailey. "Dr. Darlington said the breed is on the endangered species list. There are only a couple of thousand left."

"Really?" Jessa said. "I didn't know Canada had its own breed of horse."

"Actually, we have a couple," said Walter, warming to his subject. "Ever heard of the Newfoundland Pony?"

Jessa shook her head.

"That's another one. Barely a handful of them left. It's a real shame when we lose these old breeds. These Canadian horses were used for everything— ploughing, taking the kids to school—the old settlers, my grandfather among them, used to race them for a little entertainment!"

Jessa looked at the sturdy chestnut mare with new admiration.

"So, you could say we're looking after a real Canadian treasure," Walter grinned.

With her ribs sticking out, her swollen eye and lopped-off tail, Sienna was a most unusual-looking treasure. Jessa led her back out to her paddock and slipped her another carrot. She imagined Sienna's ancestors plowing the prairie and pulling sleighs in Quebec.

"So, Walter. Could I take you out for coffee and cheesecake down at Miranda-Lou's Café?" Mrs. Bailey asked as Jessa joined Cheryl where she sat on an upturned bucket, eating a sandwich.

Walter licked his lips and patted the space between his suspenders. He looked like he could use some cheesecake to fatten him up a bit.

Cheryl waited until the pair was out of earshot and said, "See! I told you something was going on!"

"Don't be stupid. You know how much Mrs. Bailey likes cheesecake."

"No, sorry. Didn't you see how she smiled at him? They aren't going for cheesecake. They are going on a date."

"Cheryl! You're nuts! Old people do not date. It's too undignified."

"Undignified? Come on. We're talking about Mrs. Bailey here—a woman who spits in the dirt when she gets mad."

"Who would want to date someone like that?" Jessa asked, changing her argument slightly.

"Apparently, Walter Walters."

Jessa said nothing. She bit off the last good bite of her apple and got up to take the rest to Rebel. *Time would tell*, she decided. *Once Sienna's training was finished, Walter would disappear and things would get back to normal at Dark Creek. Cheryl would just have to wait and see.*

Chapter Fourteen

All week Jessa diligently practised heeling with Romeo. And, all week Jessa carefully avoided asking her mother what would happen if nobody claimed the stray dog. It seemed to Jessa that chances were slim anyone would call now, after so long.

She figured that if she didn't ask if she could keep Romeo, her mother couldn't say 'no'.

On Friday afternoon, Jessa's mother was waiting for her when she came home from school.

"Jessa. We have to talk about the dog."

Jessa's heart sank. Not only did her mother look serious, she was holding onto Romeo by his collar. She let the dog go after Jessa had shut the kitchen door behind her.

"Oh, Romeo, what did you do now?"

"Would you like some chocolate milk?"

Whatever she had to say, Jessa decided it couldn't be good. Jessa filled a tall glass with milk and sat down opposite her mother. She tipped six heaping teaspoons into her glass and whipped her milk into a thick chocolately froth. Normally, she liked to put in ten spoonfuls, but Jessa decided not to annoy her mother.

"Something happened today while you were at school."

Jessa reached under the table and rubbed Romeo with her foot.

"I had a visit from the police."

"What!" Jessa was horrified. "What did Romeo do?" she asked, not really wanting to know the answer.

"You know Mr. and Mrs. Blakeney down the street?"

Jessa nodded glumly. That was obviously it. Somehow, Romeo had got out of the house and had chased the Blakeneys or the Blakeneys' cat or. . . . Then, an even worse thought occurred to her.

"Do they know the real owners? Did they call the police and say we stole him?"

"Jessa! Don't be silly. No, just listen. While the Blakeneys were at work, someone broke into their house. The thieves stole their stereo, TV, a camera and some jewelry."

Jessa put down her glass and stared at her mother in horror. She couldn't believe it. Nobody ever got robbed on Desdemona Street. Nothing exciting ever happened in their sleepy neighbourhood.

"The police came here because the Blakeneys told them that sometimes I'm at home in the afternoon. They wanted to know if I'd seen anything suspicious. Of course, I was actually at the office today."

"Oh, no! Did the burglars come here, too?"

"No. In fact, that's what I wanted to talk to you about. The police officer said something interesting while he was here. Apparently, houses with dogs don't get robbed nearly as often as houses without."

The spoon stopped in the air halfway to Jessa's mouth.

"So that's why we didn't get robbed?"

Under the table, she rubbed Romeo a little harder.

"Well, we don't know that for sure, but since Romeo is here, and since you seem to be looking after him quite well. . . ."

Jessa didn't even let her mother finish. She jumped up, knocking her chair over backwards. Romeo scooted out from under the table, barking excitedly.

"Thank you! Oh, thank you Mom!"

"Fine. But, if we're going to keep him, we can't leave him locked up in your room all day. That's not fair. We need to do something about fixing the fence in the backyard."

"I'll help!"

"Good. We'll start tomorrow. Would you be willing to spend a little less time at the barn this weekend?"

"Yes! Of course! Will we get him a doghouse?"

"Maybe. I thought we could cut a hole in the kitchen door and make him a special doggy entrance so he can go in and out."

"Oh, he would love that! We could keep the door closed to the dining room so he can't get at the plants again," Jessa suggested.

"Good idea. Now, young lady, finish your milk, do your homework and then take Romeo for a nice long walk. Just because he's staying, doesn't mean you can stop training him."

Jessa crouched on the floor and ruffled the collar of white fur around her dog's neck.

"Romeo! Did you hear that? You can stay!"

Romeo put his front paws on Jessa's chest and gave her cheek a big, wet lick.

"Please divide into groups of three."

Cheryl and Jessa looked for a third person to join their group. Cheryl waved at Jason and Maestro. He grinned and jogged over to join them.

"Today we are going to practise our heeling in figure eights. Two people in each group will be the posts, and the third will heel around them. You all know what a figure eight looks like, right?"

There was a little giggling and general nodding from the group of dog owners gathered at the field. "Okay, posts, take your positions."

Jessa and Cheryl maneuvered their dogs into place about four metres apart, facing each other.

Jason and Maestro heeled briskly. The fact he was walking around two sitting dogs and their owners didn't phase Maestro in the least. The first two or three times Maestro brushed past, Romeo stretched to sniff. It was almost more than he could bear to see the dog trotting past him, tail waving merrily. He couldn't quite understand why he wasn't allowed to jump up and have a good romp. Jessa glared at him fiercely. He restrained himself admirably and stayed more or less in one place.

Jessa watched Jason and Maestro as they worked, turning together, slowing down and speeding up as Rodney demanded. The young man and his dog were totally tuned in to each other. Maestro's head tilted up and he watched Jason's every move. Jason never seemed to tire of praising and encouraging his dog as they marched around and around.

When they halted for the last time, Jessa felt like applauding.

Cheryl and Ginger were next. "Talk to your dog, Cheryl," said Rodney. "I want to see that tail wagging! That's better! Now, see if you can get her to speed up as you go past Romeo—don't let her lag behind."

Rodney moved on to help another group.

Jessa and Romeo didn't manage quite so well when their turn came. Romeo wasn't paying attention as they approached Jason and Maestro. Instead of turning, Romeo kept on going straight. Jessa stumbled right over top of him and nearly crashed into Jason. Romeo yelped and Cheryl burst out laughing.

"Don't worry, Jessa. You two are doing way better than when you started."

Jessa blushed at Jason's kind words. She stopped and made Romeo sit before continuing with her figure eight. Around they went. She tried talking to him the way Jason had talked to Maestro. Romeo's ears perked up and he wagged his tail.

"That's quite good, Jessa," said Rodney, unable to completely conceal his surprise.

Jessa caught Jason smiling at her. She smiled back. For the first time since the beginning of obedience school, Jessa felt like she and her dog might actually be learning something. *Maybe,* she thought, *it was because today was the first day Romeo really was her dog, and not just a stray she was looking after for awhile.*

Chapter Fifteen

"I can't stay long today," Jessa warned when she arrived at the barn. "I think I'll give Rebel the day off so I can help you with Sienna," she said to Walter.

"Let me hold Romeo," Mrs. Bailey offered. "Why do you have to rush off?"

"Mom and I are fixing the fence because I get to keep Romeo!" Jessa still couldn't quite believe she really owned a dog. "Romeo is officially my dog," she said, as if saying it a few times in public might make it seem more real.

"Hmmmm. Well, I suppose he has settled down quite a bit since that first day he chased my hens." Mrs. Bailey glowered at Jessa. "I still wouldn't trust him off this leash."

"I know, I know," said Jessa. Then she looked at Romeo. "Sit," she said with an air of authority. Romeo sat. "Down," Jessa added for good measure. Romeo didn't hesitate. He lay on his belly at Mrs. Bailey's feet.

"Not bad," she had to admit. "Not bad at all. Jessa, don't keep Walter waiting."

Jessa slipped into the round-pen with Walter and Sienna. Walter winked at her and Jessa grinned back at the wiry old horse trainer.

"So, you ready to go riding?" he asked.

Jessa hardly had time to think, to be afraid. After a few minutes of reviewing the saddle-slapping exercise, Jessa flopped over Sienna's back. Walter led them around the pen. Sienna behaved as if she had been doing this for years.

"Jessa, I'm going to give you a leg up now. Settle on her back as gently as you can. Try not to bang her with your legs."

And then, she was up on Sienna's back. For a moment, the three of them stood frozen in the middle of the pen. Slowly, Jessa let out her breath. She could feel Sienna's tension easing away as the horse realized nothing dreadful was going to happen.

Walter rubbed her forehead and then grinned up at Jessa.

"Excellent, Jessa! Good job. Now, stay very relaxed, go with her movement when I start to lead her, don't resist in any way."

Sienna took her first step with a rider aboard. At first, she was tentative, not sure how to compensate for Jessa's weight, and her higher center of gravity now that Jessa was sitting upright.

"Good girl," Jessa crooned.

Walter led the mare slowly around the ring. He stopped and started and never let up with his gentle stream of reassuring words.

"Barbara, could you let us out, please?" he said

after fifteen minutes of slow work in the pen.

"Wait a second. Where are we going?"

"Relax, Jessa. We'll just walk down the driveway and back."

Jessa thought of Sienna on her first day at Dark Creek, the way she had raced down the driveway like a mad thing. Quickly, she replaced that picture with an image of an ancient cart horse plodding along.

Sienna chose something in between. She pranced lightly along the driveway, her head up, ears perked forward, her neck arched. At the end of the driveway, Walter stopped and let her have a nibble of grass.

Jessa reached forward and stroked Sienna's neck. The little iron horse munched happily. Heading back up the driveway towards the barn, Jessa couldn't stop smiling.

Sitting atop the horse whose past experiences might have ruined her forever, Jessa felt a huge sense of pride in the little mare's accomplishments. And, all they had done was walk slowly down the driveway and back!

Jessa dismounted at the barn and helped Walter untack.

"We'll pop a bridle on her next time," he said. "Barbara, pretty soon you won't need me around here any more." He winked at Mrs. Bailey who had handed Romeo back to Jessa and was now suddenly very interested in tidying up the grooming brushes.

"I don't suppose you have to disappear entirely,"

Mrs. Bailey said. "I mean, Sienna is hardly a fully polished mount, now is she?"

Jessa looked up from grooming Sienna. She had made Romeo lie down and he seemed quite content to rest in the shade beside the barn. Jessa swallowed hard. Mrs. Bailey seemed awfully keen to keep Walter around. *Could Cheryl have been right?*

"Hey! Come back here, you rat!" Jessa said, watching Romeo scamper off across the yard with a dandy brush in his mouth.

She and Walter gave chase, which only made Romeo run faster.

"Why wasn't he tied up?" demanded Mrs. Bailey from the sidelines as the trailing end of his leash whisked past her.

Jessa didn't stop chasing long enough to explain that she had told him to 'stay' and had assumed he would. Obviously, he had grown bored while she had been grooming Sienna and decided to create a little excitement.

"Whew!" said Walter, giving up and holding his side. "That critter can sure run!"

A minute later Jessa stopped, too. She sat down on the ground and glared at her dog. He dropped the brush and trotted over to her quite innocently. Jessa tied him up and went back to work grooming the mare.

"Well, I see those training classes are paying off," said Mrs. Bailey with a sniff.

"There's no rushing an education, Barbara. You know that." Walter nodded kindly at Jessa. "Just don't you give up on that dog of yours, Jessa."

Mrs. Bailey changed the subject abruptly. "I talked to the Animal Rescue people again this morning. I told them we would keep working with Sienna awhile longer. She's going to be a wonderful horse for someone. We may as well get the job done properly. As you say, Walter, there's no rushing an education."

Walter didn't say anything. He just nodded and smiled and then gave Sienna a friendly pat on the rump.

When Sienna had been put away and Jessa sat on the mounting block waiting for her mother to come and pick her up, she watched Mrs. Bailey and Walter walking up towards the house together. Maybe they *were* walking a little closer together than was absolutely necessary.

Jessa kneeled down beside Romeo and gave him a kiss on the nose. His pink tongue flicked out and kissed her back.

Jessa pounded a nail into the top of a new board on the back fence. She and her mother had carefully replaced all the missing and rotten planks so Romeo wouldn't be able to escape. A new latch, and the back gate was as good as new.

As they worked, Romeo lay sprawled on the grass under the shady apple tree. He didn't look like he wanted to go anywhere.

The whine of a saw cutting through the kitchen door pierced the quiet of the late afternoon. Jessa whacked at the last nail and then stood back to admire their work. It was amazing how much the two of them had managed to get done.

"Jessa? Can you come here and hold this?"

Jessa joined her mother at the back door. She held the new doggie door in position while her mother fastened it into place with screws.

"There," she said. "Jessa, go get Romeo and see how he likes it."

"Come on, Romeo," Jessa called. "Let's go!"

Slowly, Romeo roused himself from his nap. He bowed deeply, stretching and yawning.

Romeo ambled over to the kitchen door and looked at the heavy plastic flaps that hung over the new opening.

"Go inside and call him."

Jessa went into the kitchen and called.

Romeo stood outside and whined. His head tipped from side to side as he listened to Jessa's voice on the other side of the door. "Come on in, Romeo. Don't be afraid!"

Romeo barked and stared at the door. Jessa poked her head out the doggie door and Romeo jumped forward and licked her cheek. She disappeared back inside. Romeo barked and wagged his tail.

"He thinks you're playing peek-a-boo with him!" her mother laughed.

"I think I'll have to demonstrate," Jessa said, squeezing out through the little door.

Romeo pounced on her, licking her face. Jessa could hardly stop giggling. She turned around and scrambled awkwardly back through the tiny door. It was quite a squeeze!

Romeo barked twice and then plunged through the opening into the kitchen. Once he had the hang of it, he raced in and out of his new entrance, barking like a fool.

"Looks like he's enjoying himself!" said Jessa's mother.

Jessa beamed. Yes, Romeo certainly looked happy with the renovations to his new home.

Chapter Sixteen

"Fetch the brush," Jessa said, pointing at the horse brush lying on the gravel driveway. Romeo looked at her blankly. A moment earlier, Jessa had told him to sit, which was exactly what he was doing. Like a statue.

"What are you two doing?" asked Mrs. Bailey.

"I'm trying to teach him how to fetch on command. He needs a trick for the Top Dog contest. I thought that since he liked brushes so much. . . ."

Mrs. Bailey laughed. "He's always carrying things around. That should be easy!"

"That's what I thought. But look at him!"

Romeo sat looking at his owner expectantly. He wiggled his tail but showed no interest whatsoever in the brush.

"Try putting it in his mouth," suggested Mrs. Bailey.

Jessa picked up the brush and tried to make Romeo take it from her. He clenched his teeth together and pulled his head away.

She decided to try a different approach. Romeo

had learned to use his doggie door through imitation, so. . . . She tossed the brush and then ran after it saying, "Fetch, Romeo! Fetch!" She picked up the brush and showed it to her dog. Romeo lay down and put his head on his paws.

Mrs. Bailey chuckled. "That was very good, Jessa. Maybe you should compete in the Top Dog contest?"

Jessa rolled her eyes. She didn't feel like laughing. They were going to be the only ones in the whole class without any kind of fancy trick. *Why wasn't Romeo more cooperative?*

She gave up and snapped the lunge line onto his collar. The class was working on getting the dogs to come when called. Jessa knew Romeo would never be allowed to go trail riding unless he had mastered that particular skill.

Mrs. Bailey had agreed to help her with this part of the training. While Jessa made Romeo sit and stay, Mrs. Bailey cradled one of her hens in her arms. She clucked at it while Jessa walked away from Romeo to the end of the lunge line.

"I'll do a practice one first," Jessa said. "Romeo, come!"

Romeo hopped to his feet and trotted smartly to Jessa. He sat in front of her just like he was supposed to.

Jessa praised him and then made him sit and stay again.

"Ready?" she asked Mrs. Bailey.

"Are you ready Isobel?" Mrs. Bailey asked her chicken.

Isobel bobbed her head back and forth. "We're ready!"

Jessa called her dog. Mrs. Bailey let go of the chicken who darted across the driveway. Romeo ignored the hen completely and sat in front of Jessa just as he had before.

Mrs. Bailey clapped and Jessa gave her dog a huge hug. "Good dog!" she said. "What a good, good dog!"

"Keep at it, Jessa. Between Sienna and that dog of yours, I must admit you are learning a thing or two about patience and persistence."

Jessa couldn't agree more. Now, if she could just patiently get Romeo to understand retrieving, life would be just about perfect.

"Bang!" Cheryl said, shooting her imaginary gun at Ginger. The dog fell to the floor in a dead faint.

"She's going to win for sure," Jessa said grudgingly. She helped herself to two peanut butter cookies from the plate on the bright green kitchen table at Cheryl's house.

Cheryl's parents owned a little theatre company. They were always doing interesting things in the way of interior decorating. Their last play had used black backdrops spattered with blotches of green and orange paint. The leftover paint had seemed too good to waste. Luckily, the whole kitchen was painted in bright primary colours so the freshly painted table fit right in.

Jessa liked coming over after dinner for dessert at Cheryl's house.

"So, what are you going to do?" Cheryl asked.

"About what?"

"Resurrection," Cheryl said. Ginger jumped to her feet. She sat up on her hind legs and begged for a bit of cookie. Cheryl broke off a tiny piece and tossed it in the air. Ginger caught it in mid-air.

"About Sienna."

"What do you mean?" Jessa asked.

"I saw you and that horse. Are you just going to stand by and let some total stranger take her away?"

Jessa stared at the plate of cookies. As Sienna's training progressed, she found herself dreading the day she would have to say goodbye. Sienna trusted her now. Her and Walter. *What would happen if someone adopted Sienna who didn't understand her properly? Someone who didn't know how afraid she had been?*

"I don't think I can do anything about it," she said finally.

"Some attitude," Cheryl snorted. "Why don't you adopt her?"

"Me? I can't adopt her! There's no way we could afford a second horse." It was hard enough for Jessa and her mother to meet all of Rebel's expenses.

"Do you even know what it takes to adopt a horse?"

"No, not exactly," Jessa admitted.

"Come on!" Cheryl said, hopping off her stool and heading for the den.

"What are you doing?" Jessa asked.

"They must have a web page," Cheryl said,

settling in front of the computer.

"Bingo!" she said, locating the Kenwood Animal Rescue Society home page.

"Hey look, they have a questionnaire right here. It determines whether you are suitable as a potential adopting home."

"I already know I wouldn't be," Jessa said. "I live in town and don't have money for board."

"True. But Mrs. Bailey has a farm. Let's take the quiz and see if she would qualify."

Cheryl printed off a copy of the quiz and she and Jessa retreated to the kitchen to fill it out.

"'Is this your first horse?'" Cheryl read.

"Yeah, right. Mrs. Bailey has owned horses for fifty years. More, I bet."

"'Do you have the experience required to work with a green horse?'"

"Yes. Definitely."

"'If you had a training problem and needed assistance, do you know a reputable trainer who uses humane methods?'"

"Walter Walters," Jessa and Cheryl said in unison.

"'Adequate stabling?'"

"Yes."

"'Quality feed and any necessary supplements?'"

Jessa thought of how quickly Sienna was gaining weight with her new diet.

"No problem."

"'Vet's name?'"

"Dr. Darlington."

"'Farrier?'"

"Tony Frey."

"They have some rules here, too." Cheryl kept reading. "'The adopter must not abuse the horse in any way, must not allow the horse to run at large and must be prepared to cover any emergency veterinary costs which may arise.'"

"So far, so good."

"'If the prospective adopter is approved by the Kenwood Animal Rescue Society adoption committee, the new owner must agree not to sell the horse for a period of at least two years. For the first year, official ownership remains with the Rescue Society.'"

"Then what happens?"

"It says here you get inspected again and if the committee decides you're okay, they sign over the ownership papers."

Jessa didn't think Mrs. Bailey would have any trouble at all qualifying to adopt Sienna. *The question was, did Mrs. Bailey want another horse at Dark Creek Stables?*

"Somehow we need to convince Mrs. Bailey," said Cheryl, echoing Jessa's thoughts.

"Do we have time to go down there?" Cheryl asked.

"Now?"

"No time like the present. Your bike's here. If we ride fast we can get down there, talk to Mrs. Bailey and ride back—all before dark."

"Let's go," said Jessa.

Chapter Seventeen

"Oh no!" Jessa said as they scrunched to a stop beside the barn. "Walter's truck!"

Cheryl raised her eyebrows. "See? I told you. He's *always* here!"

The girls dropped their bikes on the ground and walked towards the tack room.

Jessa opened the door and then staggered backwards. She turned around and bumped into Cheryl as she tried to flee. Her eyes bulged and her face turned bright red.

"What the?! . . ." Cheryl asked.

"Howdy girls! I was just saying goodbye. Are you helping me again on the weekend Jessa? I thought we could do some work in the ring, get Sienna used to a bit and a bridle."

"Ahhh . . . errr . . . yes. Sure. Fine. Saturday."

Cheryl looked at her friend as if she had suddenly lost her mind.

Mrs. Bailey emerged from the tack room. For a change, she didn't say anything about dropping their bikes instead of putting them away in the shavings shed.

"Hello girls—lovely evening for a bike ride."

Walter climbed into his truck, nodded cheerily to Mrs. Bailey and drove away.

"What's wrong?" Cheryl mouthed to Jessa who was suddenly quite pale.

Jessa beamed her friend with a glare clearly meant to end all further questions—at least as long as Mrs. Bailey was around. Mercifully, Cheryl took the hint and temporarily swallowed her curiosity.

"Mrs. Bailey," Cheryl began. "Could we talk to you for a minute—about Sienna?"

Mrs. Bailey held up her hand. "Funny you should mention that little mare. Walter and I were talking about her over dinner."

"You were? Not about sending her back? Because Jessa and I were thinking. . . ."

Mrs. Bailey gave her head a gruff shake, not pleased at being interrupted. Jessa was glad her friend had taken over the conversation. She still didn't trust herself to speak.

"Walter has quite an interest in old breeds of horses—as you might have noticed." The girls nodded. "He has agreed to pay half of Sienna's expenses if I'll keep her here."

"Really?" Jessa managed to say.

"We thought maybe, if Dr. Darlington said it was okay, we'd breed her next year."

"Cool!" said Cheryl. "You mean Sienna might get to have a foal? Could Jessa and I name the baby?"

"Now hold on, Cheryl. None of this will happen if she's not healthy and strong enough. But the breed as a whole is in terrible trouble. Walter and I thought this could be a way we could help preserve these horses."

"In that case, you'll need this!" Cheryl pulled the somewhat rumpled adoption application form out of her back pocket. "We've already filled most of it out for you."

Cheryl handed Mrs. Bailey the form. "Thank you, girls! You must be mind readers! Jessa, I hope you'll keep working with Sienna. Walter says you have a real touch with her."

Jessa allowed herself a small smile. Then, as politely as she could, she excused herself to go and see Sienna.

Cheryl joined her a few minutes later.

"What is wrong with you?" she demanded to know once Mrs. Bailey had made her way back to the house.

Jessa swallowed hard. "Cheryl—it was awful—he . . . he. . . ."

"Spit it out!"

"He kissed her!"

"What!?"

"In the tack room—he was kissing her goodbye!"

"You mean they were lip-locked in there?"

"No," Jessa said in disgust. "He kissed her on the cheek."

"That's it?"

"Yeah, well—Mrs. Bailey took off her hat and let

104

him. She *never* takes her hat off for anyone."

The girls were quiet for a minute, watching Sienna munch her hay.

"So, maybe we're going to see lots more of Walter around here," said Cheryl.

"Especially now that Sienna is staying," said Jessa. She wasn't sure whether to be happy about this turn of events or not.

The sun was beginning to drop quickly towards the horizon. The late afternoon light brought out the rich, coppery highlights of Sienna's coat.

"She sure looks happy," said Jessa.

"So's Mrs. Bailey, I'd say," said Cheryl with a wink.

"Let's get going. I have to be home by dark," Jessa said.

Chapter Eighteen

The next day after school, Jessa cut down the back alley. Romeo had taken to waiting for her by the back gate. It was like he had a built-in clock. He seemed to know when she was due to arrive.

Today, though, he was nowhere in sight. Jessa whistled for him as she slipped in through the back gate.

"Romeo?" she called. "Come on, boy! I'm home!"

But no black nose appeared at the dog door. *That was strange,* Jessa thought. A faint tingle of fear crept up the back of her neck. *Could something terrible have happened to him?*

She tore open the back door. "Jessa. Please come in here," her mother's voice called from the living room.

Panic seized Jessa. She rushed into the living room and stopped dead. Her mother sat on the edge of the old armchair. She was not alone in the room.

A frail old woman sat on the couch, holding a

cup of tea. Romeo lay at the woman's feet, pressed as close as he could get to her thin legs.

"Jessa, this is Mrs. Chatwell. Romeo's . . . I mean, Panda's owner."

Jessa couldn't breathe. "Romeo?" she said, not believing what she was hearing. Romeo came across the living room, gave her hand a quick lick and then went back to lie down beside Mrs. Chatwell.

"No!" she said, anguished tears stinging her eyes. Jessa didn't wait to hear any more. She turned and fled out the back door, ignoring her mother's cries behind her. She pelted out the gate and down the back alley, tears hot on her cheeks.

"No! No! No!" she cried, sobbing as she ran.

Behind her, she heard a bark. Looking back, she saw the black and white dog come tearing through the gate she had left open.

Jessa didn't know what else to do so she kept running. She raced down the alley, across the street and plunged into the poplar-lined path along the edge of the farm fields at the end of her street.

She ran and ran until she could hardly breathe. Romeo ran beside her, his tail wagging furiously. He seemed to think they were just going for a lovely, fun walk.

At the end of the field, Jessa climbed over the gate and Romeo scrambled underneath. On the other side of the fence the Dark Creek Railway Trail stretched for miles in either direction. Jessa turned south and headed for Dark Creek. She would hide there until she could think of a better plan.

Jessa crouched behind a stack of hay bales. She wondered how long she could stay hidden in the hayloft before somebody found her.

"Oh, Romeo," she sniffled. Romeo licked her cheek and whined. He put his paw on her leg as if to comfort her.

Jessa's thoughts whirled in an unhappy blur. She knew she couldn't stay in the loft forever. *Why had old Mrs. Chatwell shown up now? How could she even think of taking Romeo away?*

Tempted by the sweet-smelling loose hay, Jessa lay down and pulled her sweater close. Romeo crawled beside her and rested his head on her stomach. Jessa tried hard to imagine what she would do if she lost Romeo. In her heart of hearts she knew she would do exactly what Mrs. Chatwell had done. No matter how long it took, she would keep searching until she had her dog beside her again.

"They're here!"

Jessa sat bolt upright. Someone had flicked on the light in the loft. *When had she fallen asleep?* Dream images of huddling with Romeo in a railway car receded as her mother and Mrs. Bailey came across the creaky wooden floor towards her.

Jessa burst into tears.

"Oh, Mom. I'm so sorry. I know he has to go back . . . I know he does."

Jessa's attempt at being brave dissolved into a flood of tears. She fully expected her mother to be angry, to shout at her for running away, for stealing someone else's dog.

Instead, she felt her mother's arms around her, and heard her soothing words.

"Jessa, shhhhh. It's okay. Listen to me for a minute."

Jessa sobbed even harder. She didn't want to hear what her mother had to say, that Romeo was leaving and she would never see him again.

"Romeo's not going anywhere."

Jessa's weeping just got louder. *She was not a baby! Her mother didn't need to lie. She could handle the truth.*

She struggled to get her sobs under control, to prove to her mother how mature she could be.

"Jessa, did you hear me? Romeo is going to stay with us."

Slowly, the words began to sink in.

"But . . . wh-what about M-Mrs. Chatwell?" she blubbered.

"Here," said Mrs. Bailey handing her a tissue. "Blow your nose and sit up."

Jessa straightened up and did as she was told.

"Let me tell you what happened. Nearly two months ago Mr. and Mrs. Chatwell went on a cruise vacation. They left Panda—well, Romeo—with their youngest daughter. The day after they left, he ran away."

"Where does their daughter live?" Jessa asked.

"In Victoria. Of course, she started to look for him when he went missing but two days after the cruise had started, Mr. Chatwell had a heart attack!"

"Oh no! Poor Mrs. Chatwell," Jessa sniffled. Her own problems were suddenly looking a little less serious.

"Their daughter flew to meet them in the Bahamas where Mr. Chatwell was in the hospital. The neighbour who was supposed to continue to look for the dog didn't do a very good job."

"Is Mr. Chatwell okay?" Jessa asked.

"Well, sadly, no. They did everything possible for him, but after two weeks, he passed away."

"Oh no!"

"The rest of the family lives in Toronto, so Mrs. Chatwell and the daughter who had flown to the Bahamas then went to Ontario where they held the funeral."

"That's awful!"

"Yes," her mother agreed. "But that does explain why nobody came looking for Romeo before now. Mrs. Chatwell only flew back to Victoria the day before yesterday. She called the pound yesterday and they found our report."

"But why doesn't she want Romeo back?"

Jessa couldn't imagine anyone first losing her husband and then giving away her dog.

"Mrs. Chatwell has decided to move back to Ontario, to be closer to her other children. One of her sisters also lives there. They'll be sharing an apartment, but in a building which doesn't allow pets. So, when she realized how well Romeo seemed to be doing with us, Mrs. Chatwell wanted to meet you and explain everything so you didn't think she was a horrible dog owner."

Jessa started crying again.

"*Now* why are you crying?"

"Because I was so selfish and so rude and . . . ohhhh. . . . Poor Mrs. Chatwell . . ." Jessa wailed miserably. *Mrs. Chatwell must think she was the most awful person. She didn't even deserve to have a dog!*

"Jessa! For goodness sake, pull yourself together! Mrs. Chatwell is a woman who raised four children of her own and is a grandmother eight times over. Do you think she doesn't know a thing or two about kids?"

Jessa sniffled and shrugged her shoulders. She took off her glasses and tried to wipe them off.

"She was quite worried about you when you ran off like that. So, I'd like you to go down to the tack room and phone her right now. I'm sure Mrs. Bailey won't mind."

Mrs. Bailey nodded.

"How did you know where to find me?" Jessa asked as she straightened herself up a little.

"Well, I must admit I thought you'd come back, especially when the dog chased after you like that. When you didn't, I called Cheryl's house. She figured you'd probably come here."

"Where's Mrs. Chatwell?" Jessa asked. She suddenly had a picture of the elderly woman sitting on their couch at home, her thin legs daintily crossed.

"She went back to her own house to wait to hear what happened."

Downstairs, Jessa dialed the number her mother had given her. At the other end of the line, an old woman's voice answered, "Hello?"

"Oh, hello. This is Jessa Richardson calling." Jessa thought her own voice still sounded pale and quivery. She wondered if Mrs. Chatwell could tell.

"Oh my goodness! Are you all right?"

"Yes. Yes, I'm fine. I'm sorry that I ran out . . . I just . . . well . . . I. . . ."

"You had me scared half to death! Your poor mother didn't know where you had gone!"

Jessa began to sniffle into the phone and for a moment there was total silence at the other end of the line. When Mrs. Chatwell spoke again her voice was softer.

"Well, I do understand it must have been quite a shock for you. I'm glad you are all right. And to be perfectly honest, I'm just pleased that at least I don't have to worry about Panda any more. I had such dreadful thoughts that he had been run over by a car, or was running around loose without food or shelter. I'm very glad you found him."

"Well, actually, he found us."

Mrs. Chatwell's voice shook. "You just never know what may happen, do you?"

"I'm really sorry to hear about Mr. Chatwell,"

Jessa said awkwardly. She wasn't sure whether it was polite to mention it or not.

At the other end of the line, Mrs. Chatwell sighed sadly. "Yes, it was a terrible thing. I'm very fortunate to have such a loving family to help me. I talked to Jeannie—that's my sister in Toronto— she's already fixed up the spare bedroom for me. It's so hard to see the house here without. . . ." The old woman stopped. "I'm sorry, dear. I shouldn't go on so."

"It's okay," Jessa said. "What's your new address in Toronto? Maybe I could write to you sometimes, to let you know how Romeo is doing."

"Romeo . . . you know, that's not a bad name for him. He is a sweetheart! Jessa, that would be lovely. Perhaps you could send a photograph of the two of you together. Then, when I get lonely for the little rascal, I can look at the picture and know he's happy in his new home."

Jessa agreed and wrote down Mrs. Chatwell's new address. It was dark outside when she joined Romeo and her mother out in the car.

"About ready for bed?"

Jessa nodded. Exhaustion and a huge sense of relief made her whole body slump into the seat. Her mother reached over and squeezed Jessa's hand lightly.

They drove home together quietly listening to the news on the radio and the occasional clink of Romeo's dog tags from the back seat.

Chapter Nineteen

Jessa dialed Rodney Blenkinsop's answering machine. It was the final day of classes and it was pouring with rain. Rodney wasn't there but the recorded message answered Jessa's question.

"You have reached Poochie Pals Dog Training Centre. If you are calling to find out whether classes are cancelled today due to the rain, the answer is 'No!' So, dig out your raincoat and head out to meet the rest of us at the field."

Jessa hung up without listening to the rest of the message. She sighed. So much for wishing the last class would be cancelled. At least, cancelled until Romeo had mastered some sort of trick.

For weeks she had tried to get Romeo to fetch or play dead or even sit up and beg. He still liked to carry things around when she wasn't looking, but getting him to do it on command? Forget it.

"Do you want a ride?"

"Thanks, Mom. Are you going to stay and watch?"

Her mother put on her big yellow rain slicker

and grabbed the giant umbrella from the big old metal milk can by the front door. "Are you kidding? I wouldn't miss this for the world!"

Jessa was amazed to see just about everyone from the group had shown up, despite the inclement weather.

First, Rodney marked everyone on the group exercises. All the dogs lined up and sat while their owners walked away. Jessa was so nervous, she clenched her fists into tight balls at her sides. But she was worrying for nothing. Romeo didn't try to get up or walk away.

"Return to your dogs," Rodney said when their time was up.

The whole class repeated the exercise with their dogs lying down on the wet grass. Again, Romeo did his job beautifully. Jessa's mother gave her a hug when they joined her under the big umbrella to wait for their turn to do the individual exercises.

One by one, owners put their dogs through their paces. They heeled slowly and quickly, did figure eights and called their dogs to come.

Jason and Maestro were nearly perfect—they even managed to do the figure eight exercise without a leash. Jessa clapped heartily—partly with enthusiasm and partly to keep warm. Jason did deserve the applause—he had certainly worked hard with his dog.

Cheryl's off-leash heeling didn't go quite so well. Ginger still lagged behind a bit on the corners and

Rodney gently scolded Cheryl for trying to bribe her dog with pieces of salami.

When Jessa's turn came, she gave Romeo a quick pat on the head and then began to walk briskly in a giant rectangle around Rodney.

"Halt!"

She stopped and Romeo sat smartly at her side. *So far, so good,* she thought. The rest of the heeling exercise went quite smoothly.

"Would you like to try without the leash?" Rodney asked.

Jessa looked at Romeo sitting at her side. She shrugged. *What the heck?* They had nothing to lose.

She unsnapped the leash and off they went again. Jessa kept looking down anxiously. To her amazement, Romeo stayed right at her side. Whenever she stopped, he stopped and sat—a little crookedly, perhaps, but at least he sat.

Rodney wrote something on his clipboard.

"Ready to see if he'll come when he's called?" he asked.

Jessa nodded. She left Romeo sitting and then walked away across the field.

She turned to face him and waited for Rodney's signal. The instructor raised his arm and Jessa called her dog.

Romeo stood up and bowed deeply. The rest of the class laughed and clapped. Jessa held her breath. *Would Romeo come to her or not?* He finished his stretch and trotted across the field straight towards Jessa. His sit in front of her was as straight as any of the other dogs' that day. He looked up at her expectantly and waited to see what she wanted him to do next.

"Good dog!" she said, thrilled at how well he had done.

Jessa ran back to her mother's side and sheltered from the drizzle. They hadn't been the best of the group, but they hadn't made any major mistakes either.

"In just a few minutes," Rodney announced after the last dog had finished, "we'll have the Top Dog Contest. But first, I'd like to present each of you with an official Poochie Pals Graduation Certificate."

He handed out envelopes containing personalized certificates for each dog and handler.

"And now, I have a special award for the dog and owner who have shown the most improvement since the beginning of the course. It is awfully tempting to give up when you are having a bit of trouble. If Miss Jessa Richardson had given up early on, her dog would never have managed the fine performance he showed us here today. Congratulations Romeo and Jessa!"

Jessa blushed and stepped forward to collect her prize, a gift certificate from the Kenwood Pet Store.

"And now, without further delay, the Top Dog Contest!"

The first dog to demonstrate was Miguel, a tiny Chihuahua. Dressed in a green and blue turtleneck sweater, he danced on his hind legs around a little

Mexican hat on the ground. His owner, a plump woman wearing a matching sweater, clapped her hands and whistled a jaunty tune.

The whole class joined in and clapped along as the little dog hopped around on his skinny legs.

Two dogs rolled over and a handsome collie sat up and begged. Georgette the poodle barked out the answer to '2 + 2' and was promptly rewarded with a piece of cheese.

Jessa swallowed miserably when a big black lab jumped over a small obstacle to fetch a ball. He returned the ball to his owner and dropped it gently into his hands.

The crowd was delighted when Cheryl 'shot' Ginger. She didn't even seem to mind that when she dropped to the ground her tail was lying in a puddle.

"Jason, do you and Maestro have a trick?"

Jason nodded and stepped forward, holding up a yellow Frisbee.

"We're going to do some Frisbee tricks."

Jessa stepped forward to get a better look. Suddenly, Maestro whined and began to act very strangely. He barked furiously and stood right in front of Jason. At first, Jessa thought the dog was just excited about playing with the Frisbee.

But Jason wasn't doing anything. In fact, he looked most strange. He stood quite still, staring across the field.

Maestro barked and barked. He stood in front of Jason and wouldn't let him move forwards. He stood up on his hind legs and put his paws on Jason's chest.

The Frisbee dropped to the ground at Jason's side. Maestro completely ignored it. He barked into Jason's face.

Slowly, Jason sank down to the ground.

"What's happening?" someone asked.

"Is this part of the trick?" Cheryl wanted to know.

In the next moment it was clear to everyone watching that this was no trick because Jason tipped over on his side and then his whole body went stiff. He started to jerk and twist on the ground.

There was a horrible, long silent pause when nobody moved or said anything.

"He's having a seizure!" said the man with the black lab.

"I'm a nurse!" said the woman in the blue and green sweater. She thrust her Chihuahua at Jessa's mother who took the surprised dog in her arms.

"Stand back out of the way, Jessa!"

The nurse kneeled beside Jason and took off her sweater. Gently, she folded it and placed it under his head. She loosened the top button of Jason's shirt and waved everyone back.

Jessa's heart pounded. She felt totally useless as she watched Jason's long arms and legs flailing. Behind her, someone with a cellular phone called 911.

"Will he be okay?" Jessa asked.

"I think so," her mother said, not sounding too certain herself.

What was taking the ambulance so long?

A few minutes later, she heard a siren in the distance. But by then, Jason's violent jerking had stopped. His breathing was quieter and the nurse was reassuring him.

"My name is Angela," she quietly. "You've had a seizure. You're going to be okay," she said when he groaned. She read the engraved bracelet he wore on his wrist. "Jason's an epileptic," she said to Rodney. "He'll be fine."

When the ambulance attendants arrived with a stretcher, Jason was lying quietly on his side. He seemed a little confused and couldn't talk properly.

Maestro lay silently beside him. He licked Jason's cheek when the young man opened his eyes and blinked. Weakly, Jason reached out to touch his dog. Maestro gave a low growl when one of the attendants stepped forward to help.

"It's okay, Maestro. Good dog," said Rodney who carefully led Maestro out of the way. Maestro was beside himself. He whined and barked, wanting to be with his master.

"We can't take the dog in the ambulance," said one of the attendants.

"I'll put him in my car and follow you to the hospital," Angela said. "He'll be fine," she said to everyone as she took Maestro and her own little dog to her car. The woman with the cellular phone ran after her and said something through the open window before she drove away.

As the wail of the siren faded into the distance, everyone looked awkwardly at one another. Nobody seemed quite sure what to say.

"Did you see how Maestro warned him?" Cheryl said with awe. "It was like he know what was happening, like he made Jason sit down before he had the seizure."

"Yeah, that was amazing," Jessa agreed. "Hey! I have an idea."

She ran over to where Rodney and several other students were talking about what had happened. "I think we should give Maestro the Top Dog Award," Jessa blurted out.

Everyone agreed. "Great idea Jessa," Rodney said. "He sure looked after Jason, didn't he?"

"I say we all chip in and buy a specially engraved collar for Maestro, with Jason's name and address on it so if this ever happens again, the paramedics will know where Maestro belongs," Rodney suggested.

There was another murmur of agreement from the group. Everyone dug into their wallets and made a contribution.

"I'll zip over to the mall and pick up a card and some flowers," offered Jessa's mother. "Would you mind waiting for a few minutes until I get back? That way you can all sign it."

Despite the drizzle, not one person said they would leave. Suddenly, the tricks everyone had worked so hard to perfect seemed utterly silly.

The group huddled together under a big oak tree at the edge of the field and waited for Jessa's mother to come back. They talked about what a good team Maestro and Jason made, about how shocked and frightened they had felt when Jason had collapsed.

They all fell silent when the cellular phone rang. The call was quick and to the point.

"That was Angela calling from the hospital. Apparently, Jason is fully conscious again and is going to be just fine. His doctor had changed the medication they were using to control his seizures. They have to adjust the dose but they think the new medicine will control his epilepsy quite well so this won't happen very often."

Jessa heaved a huge sigh of relief. She was first in line to sign the card for Jason and his Top Dog.

Chapter Twenty

The following Saturday morning Jessa saddled up Rebel. She was a little nervous but excited, all at the same time.

"Thanks, Romeo, you chump!" she said as he dropped a plastic currycomb at her feet. He wagged his tail and barked, inviting her to play. As usual, level-headed Rebel paid no attention to the excited dog.

"Not now, silly! I'm trying to get ready. Sit!"

Romeo sat and waited patiently while Jessa mounted up. "Okay, let's go," Jessa called as she turned Rebel and headed down the driveway.

Romeo jumped up and jogged after her, his tail wagging. He could hardly believe his good fortune. No box stall!

Jessa trotted Rebel along the side of the road and then turned onto the Railway Trail. She kept glancing behind her to make sure Romeo was following. He loped along, easily keeping up.

"Good dog!" she called.

They slowed to a walk and Jessa took a deep

breath. She relaxed and allowed the sun to warm her back as they ambled along. She had no sooner relaxed into the saddle when she saw trouble ahead on the trail.

"Oh no," she muttered. A fat, brown bunny hopped out of the bushes. Jessa glanced down at Romeo, hoping he might not see the tempting creature. It was too late. Romeo had already spotted the rabbit. He yelped and took off, plunging into the bushes after the fleeing rabbit.

"Romeo!" Jessa shouted. "Romeo, come!"

She stopped Rebel on the trail and strained to hear something. There was nothing but silence from the trees.

"Romeo! Come!" she called loudly. The bushes shook and rustled and Romeo jumped back out onto the trail.

"Good dog!" Jessa said. She hopped off Rebel and smothered her dog with kisses. She pulled half a cheese sandwich from her backpack and offered it to Romeo. He gulped it down with a grateful slurp.

"Well, you deserved that," Jessa said. Rebel lowered his head toward Romeo and snorted in approval. With a final pat and another 'Good dog!' Jessa hopped back up on her pony.

She clucked and urged him into a trot. Romeo fell in to one side and together, the three of them headed off down the trail.

Author's Note

There have always been those who have worked gently with horses, striving to understand these amazing animals on the horses' terms. Over the years, many (John Lyons, Monty Roberts, Linda Tellington-Jones, and others) have worked hard to bring awareness of the humane treatment of horses into wider public consciousness. *Sienna's Rescue* describes techniques similar to those used by some of these trainers. Such crusaders have certainly inspired me and taught me a great deal about the horse-human relationship.

Dozens of other horse people have shown me how it is possible to communicate effectively with our equine companions. But the most important teachers have been the horses themselves who have taught me more than any book, video, riding lesson or clinic.

Before trying any new training techniques with your own horse, be sure to consult a professional who can give you guidance and instruction. A good trainer will work with you and your horse to help forge a lasting partnership. NIKKI TATE

About the Author

Nikki Tate likes to write her novels about horses while her two cockatiels sit on her shoulders. For as long as she can remember, Nikki has always enjoyed reading and writing about animals. She says her job as an animal control officer with the Guelph Humane Society in Ontario was one of the most exciting and interesting she has ever had. "What other kind of job can you do where you help people train their dogs, raise families of orphaned kittens in your living room or save raccoons trapped at the very top of half-finished buildings or in the bottom of old wells?"

At university, Nikki studied the many ways companion animals can have a therapeutic effect on humans. Some animals are trained as guide dogs to help seeing-impaired people. Other animals are taken to visit people in hospitals. Horses can be companion animals, too; they often are used to help physically-challenged young people learn how to ride.

Nikki Tate rides as often as she can with her daughter. Their Vancouver Island home is filled with an assortment of creatures.

Raven's Revenge

When Jessa wins a trip for two to horse camp, she and Cheryl are so excited they can hardly think of anything else. But Camp Singing Waters is not a blissful getaway. Feuding campers, a lame horse and drafty cabins are bad enough, but should they have listened more carefully to Mrs. Bailey's ominous warnings about Dr. Rainey's experiments with witchcraft? Or, are the late night ghost stories around the campfire just fuelling their overactive imaginations?

Join Jessa, Cheryl and Rebel in **RAVEN'S REVENGE**, Book 5 of the StableMates series from Sono Nis Press.

Visit the Dark Creek Website!
http://members.home.net/ripple1/rebelhome.htm

Read all the books in the StableMates series:

Rebel of Dark Creek
Team Trouble at Dark Creek
Jessa be Nimble, Rebel be Quick
Sienna's Rescue
Raven's Revenge